Alice in Wonderland

Alice in Wonderland

Adapted for the Stage by

Eva Le Gallienne
and Florida Friebus

From Lewis Carroll's Alice in Wonderland
and Through the Looking-Glass

(As presented by Rita Hassan and the American
Repertory Theatre, April 1947)

Foreword by Eva Le Gallienne

A SAMUEL FRENCH ACTING EDITION

SAMUEL
FRENCH
FOUNDED 1830

New York Hollywood London Toronto

SAMUELFRENCH.COM

FOREWORD

It is a great joy to Miss Friebus and me, as authors of this stage version of " Alice in Wonderland " and " Through the Looking Glass," that Samuel French is presenting a new and greatly revised edition of our work. After two eminently successful productions of the play on Broadway, we decided we would like to make available a complete acting version, explaining in the fullest detail exactly how this production can be put on the stage. We feel that by the use of this book any organization with the necessary equipment at their disposal, and an adequate knowledge of stagecraft, can achieve a successful " Alice," while others not so equipped can continue, as in the past, to use their own simplified techniques.

It was not without considerable trepidation that I started work on my first " Alice " production at the Civic Repertory Theatre. I realized that the word " faithful " must be the keynote of any such venture if it were to find favor with an audience. The love that countless people feel for the " Alice " books amounts to fanaticism, and I felt a deep and solemn responsibility to Carroll, Tenniel, and the Public.

Carroll is not one of those writers for children who become " as children " themselves. He presents the problem as seen by a child, but comments upon it as an adult mathematician on a holiday. Hence the bewildering and fascinating texture of his story; half adventure, half chop-logic and shrewd caricature.

This production, therefore, is not designed *primarily* for children. The "pretty-pretty," the "cute" and the "saccharine" must be as drastically eliminated on the stage as in the books. They are by no means children's books, in the sense of being "kid-stuff"—on the contrary, it seems to me that no child could possibly appreciate or understand the wit and wisdom of their nonsensical logic. The "adventures" part of the books is of course fascinating to children; the fact of going through a looking-glass, of seeing a baby turn into a pig, of talking to caterpillars, cats and rabbits, of using flamingoes as croquet mallets, and the hundreds of other strange happenings that make Alice solemnly exclaim: "Curiouser and curiouser!" are absorbing and delightful. On the other hand, who but a grown-up could possibly appreciate the bitter truth of such a remark as: "Jam tomorow and jam yesterday, but *never* jam today!"

It seems to me that a stage presentation of "Alice," in order to be faithful to the books, must appeal equally —though for different reasons—both to children and adults.

Through the use of various devices of modern stage-craft the action is continuous, Alice never leaving the stage. I felt it important to devise a technical scheme whereby all the places and characters of Alice's dream come to her—that since we experience these adventures through her mind, she must never disappear from our sight.

The aim of my production, through synchronization of music, color and form, has been to recapture to the fullest possible extent the bizarre nature of Alice's dream-adventures.

As far as form goes, Tenniel has succeeded so utterly in his illustrations in familiarizing us with such people as the Duchess, the Cheshire Cat, the Queen of Hearts, the Mad Hatter, and such odd animals as the Dodo, and the Mock Turtle with his " large eyes full of tears," that any version of " Alice " would be unthinkable without them. He has caught to perfection the mixture of fun, irony, sense and nonsense that radiates from Carroll's book. Therefore in the production all form and line follow faithfully his masterly and famous drawings.

The colors in the dream-surroundings are strictly limited to those used in cards and chess games: Red, Black, White, Yellow and Green. The only realistic color in the production is in Alice herself and in her room before her adventures start and after they end.

In the musical score the same scheme is carried out. Alice's own theme is conventional and realistic, whereas the dream characters and dream action are accompanied by impressionistic and fantastic music.

By using men in the parts of the Queen of Hearts, and the Duchess as well as her famous pepper-loving cook, I further enhanced the grotesque quality so definitely indicated in the writing and in the Tenniel illustrations.

In making the acting version Florida Friebus and I have used *only* Carroll's dialogue. We have tried to bring in all the most famous and best-loved scenes, merely arranging them to form a whole in accordance with the demands of stage presentation, and for many months, during both productions people " from 8 to 80 " flocked to see our show.

I hope this practical acting-version will prove of help to those many organizations who wish to bring " Alice " to life on the stage. It represents much work, a considerable knowledge of stagecraft, and above all a deep love and respect for Carroll and Tenniel, whose combined genius gave the immortal " Alice " to the world.

E. LE GALLIENNE.
Westport, Connecticut. 1948.

Program of the play as produced at the Civic Repertory Theatre, 105 West 14th St., New York City, on December 12th, 1932.

ALICE IN WONDERLAND

and

THROUGH THE LOOKING GLASS

By Lewis Carroll

Adapted for the stage by Eva Le Gallienne and Florida Friebus

Music by Richard Addinsell

Production devised and directed by Eva Le Gallienne

Scenery and Costumes designed, after Tenniel, by Irene Sharaff

PART I

CHARACTERS (in the order in which they speak)

ALICE ....Josephine Hutchinson
WHITE RABBIT.......Richard Waring (Freddy Rendulic and Doris Sawyer)
MOUSE ....Nelson Welch
DODO ....Joseph Kramm
LORY ....Walter Beck
EAGLET ....Robert H. Gordon
CRAB ....Landon Herrick
DUCK ....Burgess Meredith
CATERPILLAR ....Sayre Crawley
FISH-FOOTMAN ....Tonio Selwart
FROG-FOOTMAN ....Robert F. Ross
DUCHESS ....Charles Ellis
CHESHIRE CAT ....Florida Friebus
MARCH HARE ....Donald Cameron
MAD HATTER ....Landon Herrick
DORMOUSE ....Burgess Meredith
TWO OF SPADES ....David Marks
FIVE OF SPADES ....Arthur Swensen
SEVEN OF SPADES ....Whitner Bissell
QUEEN OF HEARTS ....Joseph Schildkraut
KING OF HEARTS ....Harold Moulton
GRYPHON ....Nelson Welch
MOCK TURTLE ....Lester Scharff
COOK ....Howard da Silva
KNAVE OF HEARTS ....David Turk
CLUBS ....Jacobsen, Lloyd, Green, Dwenger
HEARTS, Tittoni, Ballantyne, Cotsworth, Pollock, Fox, Scourby, Milne, Marsden, Leonard

Program Continued

PART II

RED CHESS QUEEN ....Leona Roberts
TRAIN GUARD ....Robert H. Gordon
GENTLEMAN DRESSED IN WHITE PAPER ....Robert F. Ross
GOAT ....Richard Waring
BEETLE ....Florida Friebus
HOARSE VOICE ....David Turk
GNAT ....May Sarton
GENTLE VOICE ....Agnes McCarthy
TWEEDLEDUM ....Landon Herrick
TWEEDLEDEE ....Burgess Meredith
WHITE CHESS QUEEN ....Eva Le Gallienne
SHEEP ....Margaret Love

HUMPTY DUMPTY ....*Walter Beck*
WHITE KNIGHT ....*Howard da Silva*
HORSE { FRONT LEGS ....*Robert F. Ross*
{ BACK LEGS ....*Wm. S. Phillips*
OLD FROG ....*Sayre Crawley*
SHRILL VOICE ....*Adelaide Finch*
SINGERS ....*Ruth Wilton and Adelaide Finch*
MARIONETTES *worked by English, Beck, Snaylor, Nurenburg, Hill, Tittoni, Marsden, Bauer, Pollock, under the direction of A. Spolidoro.*

IN TWO PARTS

PART I: *Alice at home. The Looking-Glass House. White Rabbit. Pool of Tears. Caucus Race. Caterpillar. Duchess. Cheshire Cat. Mad tea party. Queen's croquet ground. By the sea. The trial.*

PART II: *Red Chess Queen. Railway carriage. Tweedledum and Twee- dledee. White Chess Queen. Wool and Water. Humpty Dumpty. White Knight. Alice crowned. Alice with the two Queens. The banquet. Alice at home again.*

Choreography by Ruth Wilton.
Assistant to Miss Le Gallienne—Nelson Welch.
Animal Heads, Masks and Marionettes by Remo Bufano.
Orchestra under the direction of Sig. Sanders.
Settings constructed by Cleon Throckmorton, Inc.
Painted by Horace Armistead.
Costumes executed by Mme. Geraud.
Flying effect arranged by Fred Schultz.
Bird Costumes by Eaves Costume Co.
Wigs by Lucien.
Shoes by Selva.

PROGRAM OF REVIVAL

at the International Theatre, New York

ALICE IN WONDERLAND

Adapted for the stage by Eva Le Gallienne and Florida Friebus; based on the Tenniel drawings; scenery designed by Robert Rowe Paddock; costumes by Noel Taylor; masks and marionettes by Remo Bufano; music by Richard Addinsell; orchestra conducted by Tibor Kozma; choreography by Ruth Wilton; entire production devised and directed by Eva Le Gallienne; presented by Rita Hassan and the American Repertory Theatre.

ALICE .. ..*Bambi Linn*
(By arrangement with David O. Selznick)
WHITE RABBIT ....*William Windom (Julie Harris)*
MOUSE ....*Henry Jones*
DODO ....*John Straub*
LORY ....*Angus Cairns*
EAGLET ....*Arthur Keegan*
CRAB ....*Don Allen*
DUCK ....*Eli Wallach*
CATERPILLAR ....*Theodore Tenley*
FIRST FOOTMAN ....*Ed Woodhead*
FROG FOOTMAN ....*Robert Rawlings*
DUCHESS ....*Raymond Greenleaf*
COOK ....*Don Allen*
CHESHIRE CAT ....*Donald Keyes*
MARCH HARE ....*Arthur Keegan*
MAD HATTER ....*Richard Waring*
DORMOUSE ....*Theodore Tenley*
TWO OF SPADES ....*Eli Wallach*
FIVE OF SPADES ....*Robert Rawlings*
SEVEN OF SPADES ....*Donald Keyes*
QUEEN OF HEARTS ....*John Becher*
KING OF HEARTS ....*Eugene Stuckmann*
KNAVE OF HEARTS ....*Frederic Hunter*
GRYPHON ....*Jack Manning*
MOCK TURTLE ....*Angus Cairns*
THREE OF CLUBS ....*John Behney*
FIVE OF CLUBS ....*Bart Henderson*
SEVEN OF CLUBS ....*John Straub*
NINE OF CLUBS ....*Thomas Grace*

PART TWO

RED CHESS QUEEN ....*Margaret Webster*
TRAIN GUARD ....*John Straub*
GENTLEMAN DRESSED IN WHITE PAPER ....*William Windom*
GOAT ....*Don Allen*
BEETLE VOICE ....*Donald Keyes*
GNAT VOICE ....*Cavada Humphrey*
GENTLE VOICE ....*Angus Cairns*
OTHER VOICES ....*Mary Alice Moore, Eli Wallace*
TWEEDLEDUM ....*Robert Rawlings*
TWEEDLEDEE ....*Jack Manning*
WHITE CHESS QUEEN ....*Eva Le Gallienne*
SHEEP ....*Theodore Tenley*
HUMPTY DUMPTY ....*Henry Jones*
WHITE KNIGHT ....*Philip Bourneuf*
HORSE { FRONT LEGS ....*Will Davis*
{ BACK LEGS ....*Charles Townely*
OLD FROG ....*Donald Keyes*
SHRILL VOICE ....*Angus Cairns*
SINGERS ....*Eloise Roehm, Rae Len*

SYNOPSIS

PART I: *Alice at home. The Looking-glass house. White Rabbit. Pool of Tears. Caucus Race. Caterpillar. Duchess. Cheshire Cat. Mad Tea Party. Queen's Croquet Ground. By the Sea. The Trial.*

PART II: *Red Chess Queen. Railway Carriage. Tweedledum and Tweedledee. White Chess Queen. Wool and Water. Humpty Dumpty. White Knight. Alice Crowned. Alice with the Two Queens. The Banquet. Alice at Home Again.*

PIANO/VOCAL SCORE:
$33.00, plus postage

OVERTURE

THE BOAT SONG

(Sung by two sopranos, with childlike voices, from the orchestra pit.)

A boat, beneath a sunny sky,
Lingering onward dreamily
In an evening of July. . . .

Long has paled that sunny sky;
Echoes fade and memories die;
Autumn frosts have slain July.

Still she haunts me, phantomwise,
Alice moving under skies
Never seen by waking eyes.

In a Wonderland she lies,
Dreaming as the summer dies,
Drifting down the stream . . .

Lingering in the golden gleam . . .
Life, what is it but a dream?

THE CURTAIN RISES

ACT ONE

Scene 1

Alice's Home

(† 1, 2, and 3. * 1.) *

ALICE is discovered curled up in the great armchair by the fireplace, talking to the black kitten she holds upright on her knees. Beside her on the floor lies a tangled ball of worsted.

ALICE

Oh, you wicked, wicked little thing! Really, Dinah ought to have taught you better manners! Now, don't interrupt me! I'm going to tell you all your faults. Number one: you squeaked twice while Dinah was washing your face this morning. Now you can't deny it, Kitty; I heard you. Number two: you pulled Snowdrop away by the tail just as I had put down the saucer of milk before her. Now for number three: you unwound every bit of worsted while I wasn't looking! That's three faults, Kitty, and you've not been punished for any of them yet. You know I'm saving up all your punishments for Wednesday week. Suppose they had saved up all my punishments! What *would* they do at the end of a year? I should be sent to prison, I suppose, when the day came. Kitty, can you play chess? Now don't smile, my dear, I'm ask-

* († Refers to Illustration Reference List, page 150, * to Production Plan, page 138.)

15

ing it seriously. Because, when we were playing just now, you watched just as if you understood it; and when I said " Check! " you purred! Well, it *was* a nice check, Kitty, and really I might have won, if it hadn't been for that nasty Knight that came wriggling down among my pieces. Kitty dear, let's pretend that you're the Red Queen! Do you know, I think if you sat up and folded your arms, you'd look exactly like her. Now do try, there's a dear! You're not folding your arms properly. I'll just hold you up to the looking glass and you can see how sulky you are! (*She does so.*) And if you're not good directly, I'll put you through into Looking-glass House. How would you like *that?* Now, if you'll only attend, Kitty, I'll tell you all my ideas about Looking-glass House. First, there's the room you can see through the glass . . . that's just the same as our drawing-room, only the things go the other way. Oh, Kitty, how nice it would be if we could only get through into Looking-glass House! I'm sure it's got, oh, such beautiful things in it! Let's pretend there's a way of getting through into it somehow, Kitty. (*She rises and climbs from the arm of the chair to the mantel.*) Let's pretend the glass has got all soft like gauze, so that we can get through. Why, it's turning into a sort of mist now, I declare. It'll be easy enough to get through. . . . (ALICE *finds that the glass is indeed like a bright, silvery mist, and she goes through it at once, as LIGHTS dim . . . [* 1a.] . . . emerging, presently, on the other side, into the Looking-glass room, LIGHTS UP.*) Oh, what fun it'll be when they see me through the glass in here, and can't get at me! (*She discovers a book lying near her on the mantel, and sits down on the mantelpiece to read it.*) It's all in some language I don't know! Why, it's a Looking-glass book, of course! And if I hold it up to the glass, the words will all go the right way again. (*She holds the book up to the glass reading, as if from its reflection. . . .*)

JABBERWOCKY

'Twas brillig, and the slithy toves
Did gyre and gimble in the wabe:
All mimsy were the borogoves,
And the mome raths outgrabe.

' Beware the Jabberwock, my son!
The jaws that bite, the claws that catch!
Beware the Jubjub bird, and shun
The frumious Bandersnatch! "

He took his vorpal sword in hand;
Long time the manxome foe he sought . . .
So rested he by the Tumtum tree,
And stood awhile in thought.

And as in uffish thought he stood,
The Jabberwock, with eyes of flame,
Came whiffling through the tulgey wood,
And burbled as it came!

One, two! One, two! And through and
The vorpal blade went snickersnack!

He left it dead, and with its head
He went galumphing back.

" And hast thou slain the Jabberwock?
Come to my arms, my beamish boy!
O frabjous day! Callooh! Callay!
He chortled in his joy.

'Twas brillig, and the slithy toves
Did gyre and gimble in the wabe;
All mimsy were the borogoves,
And the mome raths outgrabe.

It seems very pretty, but it's *rather* hard to understand! Somehow it seems to fill my head with ideas
. . . only I don't exactly know what they are! However, *somebody* killed *something:* that's clear, at any
rate. . . . (THE WHITE RABBIT *enters, right and
crosses to downstage left in front of mantel.*)

THE WHITE RABBIT

Oh, my ears and whiskers, how late it's getting!
(*He draws a watch from his pocket.*) († 4.) Oh,
dear, oh, dear, I shall be too late! (*He hurries off,
left.* ALICE *jumps down from the mantelpiece and
starts to run after the* RABBIT, *but he is no longer to
be seen.*)

SCENE 2

THE LITTLE DOOR

(† 5 and 6.   * 2)

She turns around to discover that a three-legged table has appeared suddenly, downstage right, on which rests a tiny golden key. She takes the key and looks about to see what it might belong to, and there, upstage center, is a little door, about fifteen inches high. She tries the key in the lock of the little door and to her great delight it fits. She opens the door and finds that it leads into a small passage. She kneels down and looks through.

ALICE

Oh! What a lovely, lovely garden! How I should like to get out there among the bright flowers and cool fountains! (*She tries to get her head through but it won't go.*) Well, even if my head would go through, it would be of very little use without my shoulders. Oh, how I wish I could shut up like a telescope! Everything is so out of the way here I believe I could if I only knew how to begin. (ALICE *returns to the table, and this time finds a little bottle on it [* £a]. She sets the key down on the table, and picks up the bottle. It has a paper label tied around its neck with the words " DRINK ME " printed on it in large letters.*) Surely this was not here before! (*Addressing the bottle.*) Well, it's all very well to say " Drink Me," but I'll look first and

see whether you're marked "poison" or not. For
if a little girl drinks from a bottle marked "poison"
it is almost certain to disagree with her sooner or
later. (*She examines it.*) No, it must be all right.
(*She tastes it.*) Mmm! It has a mixed flavor of
cherry-tart, custard, pineapple, roast turkey, toffy,
and hot buttered toast! (*She drinks it, and as she
drinks, it seems that she is growing very small for the
table top gets high above her head.*) (* 2b.) What
a curious feeling! I must be shutting up like a telescope! I am! I wonder if I'm going out altogether,
like a candle! (*The table stops.* ALICE *runs at once
to the little door* [* 2c]. *Now she is just the right
size to go through it, but alas! She has left the key
on top of the table.*) The key! The key! (*She
runs back to the table to get the key, but it is high
above her head, and try as she will, she cannot reach
it. She starts to cry.*) Come, there's no use in crying like this! I advise you to leave off this minute!
(*She stops crying, and notices for the first time a
little cake lying under the table* [* 2a]. *She picks
it up and reads the words that are marked on it in
currants.*) Eat me! Well, I'll eat it, and if it makes
me grow larger I can reach the key, and if it makes
me smaller I can creep under the door, so either way
I'll get into the garden. (*She eats a little, and puts
her hand anxiously on top of her head to see which
way she is growing. Finding that she remains the
same size, she sets to work and finishes the cake.
Suddenly she starts to grow very fast. The table
top gets down around her knees.*) Curiouser and

curiouser! (*She picks up the little key, and hurries off to the garden door* [* 2d] *which is now so small that it's as much as she can do to look through it with one eye. She cries again as she returns to the table and puts down the key.*) You ought to be ashamed of yourself, a great girl like you, to go on crying in this way. Stop this moment I tell you! (*Suddenly there is a pattering of little feet, and the* WHITE RABBIT *returns, with a pair of white kid gloves in one hand, and a large fan in the other. He trots across, from left to right, in a great hurry, muttering to himself.*)

THE WHITE RABBIT

Oh, the Duchess, the Duchess! Oh, won't she be savage if I've kept her waiting! (ALICE *runs up behind him.*)

ALICE

If you please, sir . . . (THE WHITE RABBIT *starts violently, drops his fan, and skurries off, right.* ALICE *picks up the fan and fans herself with it as she talks. She does not notice that as she does so the table top is slowly getting higher above her head than ever.*) Dear, dear! How queer everything is today! And yesterday things went on just as usual. I wonder if I've changed in the night. Let me think: was I the same when I got up this morning? I almost think I can remember feeling a little different. But if I'm not the same, the next question is, Who in the world am I? I'm sure I can't be Mabel for I know all sorts of things, and she, oh! she knows such a very little.

I'll try if I know all the things I used to know.

> How doth the little crocodile
> Improve his shining tail,
> And pour the waters of the Nile
> On every golden scale.
>
> How cheerfully he seems to grin,
> How neatly spreads his claws,
> And welcomes little fishes in
> With gently smiling jaws!

Oh, dear! I'm sure those are not the right words. I must be Mabel after all! (*She sees the table's new height for the first time.*)   Good Heavens! There's not more than three inches left of me! It must be the fan! (*She throws away the fan. The table stops and vanishes off right.*)   (* *2e.*)   That was a narrow escape! Now for the garden! (*She runs with all speed back to the little door* [* *2c*] *but it is shut again and she has left the key on top of the table as before.*)   The key! The key! (ALICE *returns to get the key, but the table has vanished altogether, and she cries louder than ever.*)   Oh, dear! Oh, dear! Things are worse than ever. I declare it's too bad. that it is!

SCENE 3

The Pool of Tears

(† 7 and 8.   * 3)

Suddenly her foot slips, and ALICE *finds herself up to her chin in the pool of tears that she had wept when she was tall.*

ALICE

I wish I hadn't cried so much! (*She swims about trying to find her way out.*) I shall be punished for it now, I suppose, by being drowned in my own tears. (*Enter the* MOUSE, *swimming on from the right, and paddling right past* ALICE, *quite as though he doesn't see her.*) († 8.) Would it be of any use now to speak to this mouse? Everything is so out-of-the-way here that I should think very likely it can talk: at any rate there's no harm in trying. O, Mouse, do you know the way out of this pool? I am very tired of swimming about here, O, Mouse. (*Aside.*) I'm sure that must be the best way to address a mouse. I remember at school brother's Latin Grammar said, " A mouse . . . of a mouse . . . to a mouse . . . a mouse . . . O, mouse! " (*The* MOUSE *looks at her rather inquisitively and seems to blink with one of its little eyes, but says nothing.*) Perhaps it doesn't understand English. I dare say it's a French Mouse, come over with William the Conqueror. (*Aloud.*) Ou est ma chatte? (*The* MOUSE *gives a sudden leap out of the water, and seems to quiver all over with fright.*)   Oh, I beg your pardon.   I quite forgot you didn't like cats.

MOUSE (*in a shrill, passionate voice*)
Would you like cats if you were me?

ALICE

Well, perhaps not.   (*In a soothing tone.*)   Don't be angry about it.   And yet I wish I could show you our cat Dinah: I think you'd take a fancy to cats if you could only see her.   She is such a dear quiet thing . . . (*she swims lazily, backstroke*) and she's such a capital one for catching mice . . . (*The* MOUSE *gives a little shriek and bristles all over.*) Oh, I beg your pardon!   We won't talk about her any more if you'd rather not.

MOUSE

We, indeed!   As if I would talk on such a subject! Our family always *hated* cats: nasty, low, vulgar things!   Don't let me hear the name again!

ALICE

I won't indeed. (*Changing the subject.*)   . . . Are you fond . . . of . . . of dogs? There is such a nice little dog near our house I should like to show you. A little bright-eyed terrier.   It belongs to a farmer, you know, and he says it's so useful it's worth a hundred pounds!   He says it kills all the rats and . . . (*The* MOUSE *makes a commotion, and swims away from her as hard as he can go.*)   Oh, dear!   I'm afraid I've offended it again!   (*She calls after it softly.*)   Mouse dear!   Do come back again, and we won't talk about cats or dogs either, if you don't like them.   (*The* MOUSE *swims cautiously back.*)

MOUSE (*in a low, trembling voice*)

Let us get to shore and then I'll tell you my history, and you'll understand why it is I hate cats and dogs. (ALICE *and the* MOUSE *step slowly out of the water* [*see* * 4], *moving towards left, as the* DUCK, DODO, LORY *and* EAGLET *enter from the right, and downstage left, the* CRAB.)

SCENE 4

THE CAUCUS RACE

(† 9 and 10.   * 4)

As the party reaches the " shore," ALICE *squeezes the water out of her dress, and the* BIRDS, *all wet and cross, flutter and squawk uncomfortably.*

MOUSE

Now sit down, all of you, and listen to me! I'll soon make you dry enough. (*They all sit down at once, in a large ring, with the* MOUSE *in the middle.*) Ahem! Are you all ready? This is the driest thing I know. Silence all round, if you please! William the Conqueror, whose cause was favored by the Pope, was soon submitted to by the English who wanted leaders, and had been of late much accustomed to usurpation and conquest. Edwin and Morcar, the Earls of Mercia and Northumbria ——

LORY

Ugh! (*Shivering.*)

MOUSE

I beg your pardon.   (*Frowning but very polite.*) Did you speak?

LORY

Not I.

MOUSE

I thought you did. I proceed. Edwin and Morcar, the Earls of Mercia and Northumbria, declared for him, and even Stigand, the patriotic archbishop of Canterbury, found it advisable ——

DUCK

Found *what?*

MOUSE

Found *it.* (*Rather crossly.*) Of course you know what " it " means.

DUCK

I know what " it " means well enough. When I find a thing, it's generally a frog or a worm. The question is, what did the archbishop find?

MOUSE

—found it advisable to go with Edgar Atheling to meet William and offer him the crown. William's conduct at first was moderate. But the insolence of his Normans —— (*Turning to* ALICE.) How are you getting on now, my dear?

ALICE

As wet as ever; it doesn't seem to dry me at all.

DODO (*rising to his feet*)

In that case I move that the meeting adjourn for the immediate adoption of more energetic remedies ——

EAGLET

Speak English! I don't know the meaning of half those long words, and what's more I don't believe you do either. (*He bends down his head to hide a smile. Some of the other birds titter audibly.*)

DODO (*in an offended tone*)

What I was going to say was that the best thing to get us dry would be a Caucus-race.

ALICE

What *is* a Caucus-race?

DODO

Why, the best way to explain it is to do it. (*He marks out a race-course in a sort of circle.*) The exact shape doesn't matter. (*They start the race from wherever they are standing, run when and where they like. At one point the* DODO *does a stately pirouette, which seems to turn them all around, and they start in the other direction. Then, suddenly, the* DODO *calls out.*) The race is over.

LORY (*crowding around*)

But who has won?

DODO (*thinks a moment with his finger pressed to his*

*forehead in the position one sees pictures of Shake-
speare then says:*)
Everybody has won, and *all* must have prizes.

SEVERAL

But who is to give the prizes?

DODO

Why, *she*, of course. (*Points finger at* ALICE.)

ALL (*crowding around her*)

Prizes! Prizes! (ALICE *has no idea what to do but
suddenly finds a box of comfits in her pocket and
hands one to each.*)

MOUSE

But she must have a prize herself, you know.

DODO

Of course. What else have you got in your pocket?

ALICE

Only a thimble.

DODO

Hand it over here. (*They all crowd round while the*
DODO *presents the thimble.*) We beg your acceptance
of this elegant thimble. (*All cheer.* ALICE *bows in
accepting the thimble. All eat comfits with some
noise and confusion.*)

ALICE (*to the* MOUSE)

You promised to tell me your history, you know, and
why it is you hate—C's and D's.

MOUSE (*turning to* ALICE *and sighing*)

Mine is a long and a sad tale. (*Takes up his tail.*)

ALICE

It *is* a long tail, certainly. (*She looks with wonder at the* MOUSE'S *tail.*) But why do you call it sad?

MOUSE (*reads as if words were written on his tail, tossing a bit of it away at the end of each couplet, somewhat in the manner of reading a ticker-tape*)

" Fury said to
　　a mouse, That
　　　he met in the
　　　　house, ' Let
　　　　　us both go
　　　　　　to law: I
　　　　　　　will prose-
　　　　　　　cute *you.* —
　　　　　　Come, I'll
　　　　　take no de-
　　　　nial: We
　　　must have
　　the trial;
　For really
this morn-
ing I've
nothing
to do.'
Said the
　mouse to
　　the cur,
　　　' Such a

trial, dear
sir, With
no jury
or judge,
would
be wast-
ing our
breath.'
' I'll be
judge,
I'll be
jury,'
said
cun-
ning
old Fury.
' I'll
try
the
whole
cause,
and
con-
demn
you to
death.' "

(*To* ALICE *severely*.)   You are not attending!

ALICE

I beg your pardon, you had got to the fifth bend, I think?

MOUSE

I had *not*.

ALICE

A knot! Oh, do let me help to undo it!

MOUSE

I shall do nothing of the sort. (*He tosses the end of his tail over his shoulder as if it were a cloak and stalks off.*)

LORY

What a pity it wouldn't stay!

ALICE

I wish I had our Dinah here, I know I do! She'd soon fetch it back!

LORY

And who is Dinah, if I might venture to ask the question?

ALICE

Dinah's our cat. And she's such a capital one for catching mice, you can't think! And, oh, I wish you could see her after the birds! Why, she'll eat a little bird as soon as look at it. (*This causes a sensation. Some of the birds hurry off at once. But the* LORY *gathers himself up carefully.*)

LORY

I really must be getting home. The night air doesn't suit my throat. (*All the birds exit right; the* CRAB *left.*)

ALICE (*is left alone*)

I wish I hadn't mentioned Dinah! Nobody seems to like her here, and I'm sure she's the best cat in the world. Oh, my dear Dinah, I wonder if I shall ever see you any more! (THE WHITE RABBIT *enters right.*)

THE WHITE RABBIT

The Duchess! The Duchess! Oh, my dear paws! Oh, my fur and whiskers! She'll get me executed as sure as ferrets are ferrets! Where can I have dropped them? (ALICE *begins looking about. The* RABBIT *is looking about, too. They follow a figure eight pattern in their search. Presently they meet, and he* RABBIT *sees* ALICE *for the first time.*) Why, Mary Ann, what *are* you doing out here? Run home this minute and fetch me a pair of gloves and a fan! Quick now! (*The* RABBIT *runs off left. BLACKOUT.* ALICE *moves forward into right pinspot.*) (✱ 5a.)

ALICE

He took me for his housemaid! How surprised he'll be when he finds out who I am! But I'd better take him his fan and gloves . . . that is if I can find them. (*She turns . . .*)

SCENE 5

THE MUSHROOM

(† 11 and 12. ✱ 5)

. . . *and is discovered again, as the LIGHTS come up, against a background of flowers and woodland,*

*stretched on tiptoe, peeping over the edge of a large
mushroom, left, on which sits the* CATERPILLAR *with its
arms folded, quietly smoking a long hookah, and taking
not the smallest notice of herself or anything else.   To
the right is the door of the* DUCHESS' *house.   At last the*
CATERPILLAR *takes the hookah out of its mouth.*

CATERPILLAR *(after a pause)*

Who are you?

ALICE

I—I hardly know, sir, just at present.   At least I
know who I was when I got up this morning, but I
must have changed several times since then.

CATERPILLAR

What do you mean by that?   Explain yourself.

ALICE

I can't explain myself, I'm afraid, sir, because I'm
not myself, you see.

CATERPILLAR

I don't see.

ALICE

I'm afraid I can't put it any more clearly, for I can't
understand it myself to begin with, and being so many
different sizes in a day is very confusing.

CATERPILLAR

It isn't.

ALICE

Well, perhaps you haven't found it so yet.   But when

you have to turn into a chrysalis—you will some day, you know—and then after that into a butterfly, I should think you'll feel it a little queer, won't you?

CATERPILLAR

Not a bit.

ALICE

Well, perhaps your feelings may be different. All I know is, it would feel very queer to *me*.

CATERPILLAR

You! Who are you?

ALICE (*controlling her temper*)

I think you ought to tell me who you are first.

CATERPILLAR

Why? (ALICE *cannot answer, so she turns to go.*) Come back! I've something important to say. (ALICE *turns back and waits expectantly.*) Keep your temper!

ALICE (*swallowing her anger*)

Is that all?

CATERPILLAR

No. (*He draws a few leisurely puffs from his pipe, and then removes it from his mouth, preparatory to entering into a real conversation.*) So you think you're changed, do you?

ALICE

I'm afraid I am, sir. I can't remember things as I used, and I don't keep the same size for ten minutes together.

CATERPILLAR

Can't remember what things?

ALICE

Well, I've tried to say, "How doth the little busy bee," but it all came different.

CATERPILLAR

Repeat. "You are old, Father William."

ALICE (*folding her hands*)

"You are old, Father William," the young man said,
  "And your hair has become very white;
And yet you incessantly stand on your head—
  Do you think, at your age, it is right?"

"In my youth," Father William replied to his son,
  "I feared it would injure the brain;
But now that I'm perfectly sure I have none,
  Why, I do it again and again."

"You are old," said the youth, "and your jaws are
    too weak
  For anything tougher than suet;
Yet you finished the goose, with the bones and the
    beak,
  Pray, how did you manage to do it?"

"In my youth," said his father, "I took to the law,
  And argued each case with my wife;
And the muscular strength which it gave to my jaw
  Has lasted the rest of my life."

CATERPILLAR (*after a pause*)

That is not said right.

ALICE

Not quite right, I'm afraid. Some of the words have got altered.

CATERPILLAR

It is wrong from beginning to end. (*There is a moment's pause. He puffs on the hookah.*) What size do you want to be?

ALICE. Oh, I'm not particular as to size. Only one doesn't like changing so often, you know.

CATERPILLAR

I *don't* know—are you content now?

ALICE

Well, I should like to be a *little* larger, sir, if you wouldn't mind; three inches is such a wretched height to be.

CATERPILLAR (*rearing up*)

It is a very good height indeed!

ALICE

(*Piteously.*) But I'm not used to it.

CATERPILLAR

You'll get used to it in time. (*He gets down off the mushroom and crawls away, remarking as he goes:*) One side will make you grow taller, and the other side will make you grow shorter.

ALICE (*to herself*)

One side of what? The other side of what?

CATERPILLAR

Of the mushroom. (*He crawls off, left.* ALICE *walks*

around the mushroom trying to make out which are the two sides of it. Finally she reaches around its edge, and appears to take a bit in each hand.)

ALICE

Now which is which? (*Suddenly the* FISH-FOOTMAN *comes hurrying on from the left, carrying a letter almost as large as himself. He raps loudly at the door of the* DUCHESS' *house. The moment she sees him,* ALICE *hides behind the mushroom, and peering out from behind its stem, watches curiously. The door is opened by the* FROG-FOOTMAN, *who comes forward onto the first step of the house.*)

FISH-FOOTMAN (*handing him the letter*)
For the Duchess. An invitation from the Queen to play croquet.

FROG-FOOTMAN

From the Queen. An invitation for the Duchess to play croquet. (*They bow very low till their curls are almost entangled. The* FISH-FOOTMAN *then exits smartly, left, and the* FROG-FOOTMAN *places the letter on the upstage side of the house, sits down on the steps, and stares at the sky.* ALICE *goes up to the door of the house and knocks.*) There's no sort of use in knocking, and that for two reasons. First, because I'm on the same side of the door as you are; secondly, because they're making such a noise inside no one could possibly hear you.

ALICE
Please then, how am I to get in?

FROG-FOOTMAN (*staring always at the sky*)

There might be some sense in your knocking if we had the door between us. For instance, if you were inside you might knock and I could let you out, you know.

ALICE

How am I to get in?

FROG-FOOTMAN

I shall sit here until tomorrow. (*The door of the house opens and a plate grazes by the* FROG-FOOT-MAN'S *head—the door slams shut.*) Or next day maybe.

ALICE

But how am I to get in?

FROG-FOOTMAN

Are you to get in at all? That's the first question, you know.

ALICE

It's really dreadful the way these creatures argue. It's enough to drive one crazy!

FROG-FOOTMAN

I shall sit here on and off for days and days.

ALICE

But what am I to do?

FROG-FOOTMAN

Anything you like. (*He begins to whistle.*)

ALICE

Oh, there's no use in talking to him. He's perfectly

idiotic! (*She opens the door and goes through it.
BLACKOUT.*)

SCENE 6

THE DUCHESS' KITCHEN

(† 13. • 6)

*As LIGHTS come up we discover that the door leads
right into a large kitchen, in the middle of which sits the
DUCHESS, with the BABY in her lap. To the right is a
stove on which the COOK is stirring a large cauldron that
seems to be full of soup. Into the soup she continually
shakes great quantities of pepper. Near her on the
hearth sits the CHESHIRE CAT grinning broadly.*

ALICE

There's certainly too much pepper in that soup.
(*She sneezes.*) Please, would you tell me why your
cat grins like that?

DUCHESS. It's a Cheshire Cat and that's why. Pig!
(ALICE *jumps at this, but sees it is meant for the*
BABY.)

ALICE

I didn't know that Cheshire Cats always grinned. In
fact, I didn't know that cats could grin.

DUCHESS

They all can and most of 'em do.

ALICE (*pleased to have got into a real conversation*)
I don't know of any that do.

DUCHESS
You don't know much, and that's a fact. (*The* COOK *begins throwing kitchen utensils at the* DUCHESS *and the* BABY, *but the* DUCHESS *takes no notice, and it is impossible to tell whether the blows hurt the* BABY *or not.*)

ALICE
Oh, *please* mind what you're doing. Oh, there goes his precious nose!

DUCHESS
If everybody minded their own business the world would go around a deal faster than it does.

ALICE
Which would not be an advantage. Just think what work it would make with the day and the night. You see, the earth takes twenty-four hours to turn round on its axis . . .

DUCHESS
Talking of axes—Chop off her head! (ALICE *looks anxiously at the* COOK, *who is too busy stirring the soup to bother.*)

ALICE
Twenty-four hours, I *think*, or is it twelve?

DUCHESS
Oh, don't bother *me!* I never could abide figures. (*She turns her attention to the* BABY, *singing it this*

lullaby, and giving it a violent shake at the end of
each line . . .)

> " Speak roughly to your little boy
> And beat him when he sneezes,
> He only does it to annoy
> Because he knows it teases."

CHORUS (*in which the* COOK *and the* BABY *join*)
> " Wow! Wow! Wow!"

DUCHESS

> I speak severely to my boy—
> I beat him when he sneezes;
> For he can thoroughly enjoy
> The pepper when he pleases."

CHORUS

> " Wow! Wow! Wow!"

DUCHESS

Here, you may nurse it a bit if you like. (*She throws
the* BABY *at* ALICE.) I must go and get ready to play
croquet with the Queen. (*She exits, left. The* COOK
throws a frying pan after her. BLACKOUT, as
ALICE *brings the* BABY *to pinspot, right.*)

ALICE

If I don't take this child away with me, they'll surely
kill it in a day or two. Wouldn't it be murder to
leave it behind? (*The* BABY *grunts.*) Don't grunt!
That's not at all the proper way of expressing yourself. (*It grunts again.*) If you're going to turn into
a pig, my dear, I'll have nothing more to do with you.
(*There is a moment's BLACKOUT* [* 6a], *and when*

the LIGHTS come up again the BABY *is no more nor less than a pig.*)   († *14.*)   Now what am I going to do with this creature when I get it home?   (*Feeling it would be quite absurd for her to carry it any further, she sets the little creature down, center, and it trots off, right.*) If it had grown up it would have been a dreadfully ugly child.   But it makes a rather handsome pig, I think.

SCENE 7

The Cheshire Cat

(† 15 and 16. * 7)

ALICE *suddenly finds herself standing near a large tree, and is a little startled when, presently, the* CHESHIRE CAT *appears on one of its boughs* (* *7a*).

CHESHIRE CAT (*as it appears*)

Prrrraiow . . . eaiouw.

ALICE

Cheshire Puss, would you tell me, please, which way I ought to walk from here?

CHESHIRE CAT

That depends a good deal on where you want to get to.

ALICE

I don't much care where . . .

CHESHIRE CAT

Then it doesn't matter which way you walk.

ALICE

So long as I get *somewhere*.

CHESHIRE CAT

Oh, you're sure to do that if you only walk long enough.

ALICE

What sort of people live about here?

CHESHIRE CAT

To the right lives a Hatter. To the left lives a March Hare. Visit either you like. They're both mad.

ALICE

But I don't want to go among mad people.

CHESHIRE CAT

You can't help that. We're all mad here. I'm mad You're mad.

ALICE

How do you know that I'm mad?

CHESHIRE CAT

You must be or you wouldn't have come here. Do you play croquet with the Queen today?

ALICE

I should like it very much but I haven't been invited yet.

CHESHIRE CAT

You'll see me there. (*It vanishes.* ALICE *stands looking at the place where it has been. It reappears.*)

By-the-bye, what became of the baby? I'd nearly forgotten to ask.

ALICE

It turned into a pig.

CHESHIRE CAT

I thought it would. (*It vanishes.* ALICE *waits a little, and then turns to go, when suddenly it reappears again.*) Did you say pig or fig?

ALICE

I said pig. And I wish you wouldn't keep appearing and vanishing so suddenly: you make one quite giddy.

CHESHIRE CAT

All right. (*This time it vanishes quite slowly, beginning with the end of its tail, and ending with the grin, which remains after the rest of it has gone. BLACKOUT as* ALICE *moves into right pinspot.*)

ALICE

Well, I've often seen a cat without a grin, but a grin without a cat! It's the most curious thing I ever saw in all my life! I've seen Hatters before. The March Hare will be much the most interesting, and perhaps as this is May, it won't be raving mad . . . at least not as mad as it was in March.

SCENE 8

THE MAD TEA PARTY

(† 17, 18, and 19.   * 8)

ALICE *turns, as LIGHTS come up, to find a table set under a tree, and the* MARCH HARE *and the* MAD HATTER *having tea at it. The* DORMOUSE *is asleep between them. It is a very large table, but the* HARE, *the* HATTER, *and the* DORMOUSE *are crowded together at one corner of it, with a large teapot in front of them. The* HARE *and the* HATTER *are using the* DORMOUSE *as a cushion, resting their elbows on it and talking over its head.*

ALICE

It must be very uncomfortable for the Dormouse, only as it's asleep, I suppose it doesn't mind. (*Moves toward table.*)

MARCH HARE and MAD HATTER

No room—no room!

ALICE

There's plenty of room! (*She seats herself in a large armchair at the head of the table.*)

MARCH HARE (*encouragingly*)

Have some wine.

ALICE

I don't see any wine.

MARCH HARE

There isn't any.

ALICE

Then it wasn't very civil of you to offer it.

MARCH HARE

It wasn't very civil of you to sit down without being invited.

ALICE

I didn't know it was your table. It's laid for a great many more than three.

MAD HATTER (*who has been staring steadily at* ALICE *ever since her arrival*)

Your hair wants cutting.

ALICE

You should learn not to make personal remarks. It's very rude.

MAD HATTER (*the* HATTER *opens his eyes very wide at this.*)

Why is a raven like a writing desk?

ALICE (*to herself*)

Come, we shall have some fun now. I'm glad they've begun asking riddles. (*Aloud.*) I believe I can guess that!

MAD HATTER

Do you mean you think you could find out the answer to it?

ALICE

Exactly so.

MARCH HARE

Then why don't you say what you mean?

ALICE

I do. At least—at least I mean what I say. That's
the same thing, you know.

MAD HATTER

Not the same thing a bit. Why, you might just as
well say that " I see what I eat " is the same thing as
" I eat what I see."

MARCH HARE

You might just as well say that " I like what I get "
is the same thing as " I get what I like."

DORMOUSE (*sleepily*)

You might just as well say that " I breathe when I
sleep " is the same thing as " I sleep when I breathe."

MAD HATTER

It is the same thing with you. (*Silence.* ALICE *tries
to concentrate on ravens and writing desks. The
HATTER takes his watch out of his pocket and examines it and the HARE nibbles at a piece of bread
and butter he holds between his paws, like a carrot.
The* DORMOUSE *sleeps on. The* HATTER *shakes his
watch and listens to it.*) What day of the month is
it?

ALICE

The fourth.

MAD HATTER (*sighing*)

Two days wrong! (*Angrily.*) I told you butter
wouldn't suit the works.

MARCH HARE (*meekly*)

It was the best butter.

MAD HATTER

Yes, but some crumbs must have got in as well. You should not have put it in with the bread knife.

(*The* HARE *takes the watch and examines it gloomily. He dips it in his cup of tea, and looks at it again.*)

MARCH HARE

It was the *best* butter.

ALICE (*who has been looking over the* HARE's *shoulder*)

What a funny watch! It tells the days of the month and doesn't tell what o'clock it is.

MAD HATTER (*snatching it back*)

Why should it? Does your watch tell what year it is?

ALICE

Of course not. But that's because it stays the same year for such a long time together.

MAD HATTER

Which is just the case with mine.

ALICE (*politely, puzzled*)

I don't quite understand you.

MAD HATTER

The Dormouse is asleep again. (*He pours a little tea on its nose.*)

DORMOUSE

Of course, of course. Just what I was going to re- mark myself.

MAD HATTER (*to* ALICE)

Have you guessed the riddle yet?

ALICE

No. I give it up. What's the answer?

MAD HATTER

I haven't the slightest idea.

MARCH HARE

Nor I.

ALICE

I think you might do something better with the time than wasting it in asking riddles that have no answers.

MAD HATTER

If you knew time as well as I do, you wouldn't talk about wasting *it*, it's *him*.

ALICE

I don't know what you mean.

MAD HATTER (*contemptuously*)

Of course you don't. I daresay you never even spoke to Time.

ALICE

Perhaps not. But I know I have to beat Time when I learn music.

MAD HATTER

Ah! That accounts for it. He won't stand for beating. Now if you only kept on good terms with him, he'd do almost anything you liked with the clocks. For instance, suppose it were nine o'clock in the morning, just Time to begin lessons, you'd only have to

whisper a hint to Time, and round goes the clock in
a twinkling. Half-past one! Time for dinner.

MARCH HARE (*to himself*)
I only wish it was!

ALICE
That would be grand certainly, but then I shouldn't
be hungry for it, you know.

MAD HATTER
Not at first perhaps. But you could keep it to half-
past one as long as you liked.

ALICE
Is that the way *you* manage?

MAD HATTER (*mournfully*)
Not I. We quarreled last March—just before he
went mad, you know. (*Indicating the* HARE *with his
teaspoon.*) It was at the great concert given by the
Queen of Hearts, and I had to sing
   " Twinkle, twinkle, little bat,
    How I wonder what you're at."
You know the song, perhaps.

ALICE
I've heard something like it.

MAD HATTER
It goes on, you know, in this way—
   " Up above the world you fly
   Like a tea-tray in the sky.
    Twinkle, twinkle ——"

DORMOUSE (*singing in his sleep*)

Twinkle, twinkle, twinkle, twinkle. (*He continues till he's pinched.*)

MAD HATTER

Well, I'd hardly finished the first verse —— (*He pauses for the* DORMOUSE *to finish. Louder.*) I'd hardly finished the first verse. ("*Twinkle*" *continues, louder still, as he and the* HARE *pinch the* DORMOUSE *on each word.*) *I'd hardly finished the first verse*—(*the* DORMOUSE *stops*) when the Queen bawled out, " He's murdering the Time. Off with his head."

ALICE

How dreadfully savage!

MAD HATTER

And ever since that he won't do a thing I ask. It's always six o'clock now.

ALICE (*brightly*)

Is that the reason so many tea things are put out here?

MAD HATTER

Yes, that's it. It's always tea time and we've no time to wash the things between whiles.

ALICE

Then you keep moving around, I suppose.

MAD HATTER

Exactly so. As the things get used up.

ALICE

But when you come to the beginning again?

MARCH HARE

Suppose we change the subject. I'm getting tired of this. I vote the young lady tells us a story.

ALICE (*alarmed*)

I'm afraid I don't know one.

MARCH HARE and **MAD HATTER**

Then the Dormouse shall. (*They pinch him.*) Wake up, Dormouse.

DORMOUSE

I wasn't asleep. I heard every word you fellows were saying.

MARCH HARE

Tell us a story.

ALICE

Yes, please do!

MAD HATTER

And be quick about it or you'll be asleep before it's done.

DORMOUSE (*hurriedly*)

Once upon a time there were three little sisters, and their names were Elsie, Lacie, and Tillie; and they lived at the bottom of a well.

ALICE

What did they live on?

DORMOUSE (*after a deep thought*)

They lived on treacle.

ALICE (*gently*)

They couldn't have done that, you know. They'd have been ill.

DORMOUSE

So they were——very ill!

ALICE

But why did they live at the bottom of a well?

MARCH HARE (*earnestly to* ALICE)

Take some more tea.

ALICE

I've had nothing yet, so I can't take more.

MAD HATTER

You mean you can't take less. It's very easy to take more than nothing.

ALICE

Nobody asked your opinion.

MAD HATTER

Who's making personal remarks now?

(ALICE *looks offended and pours herself some tea. Then, ignoring the* HATTER, *she says sweetly to the* DORMOUSE:)

ALICE

Why did they live at the bottom of a well?

DORMOUSE

It was a treacle well.

ALICE

There's no such ——

MARCH HARE and MAD HATTER

Sh! Sh!

DORMOUSE (*sulkily*)

If you can't be civil, you'd better finish the story yourself.

ALICE

No, please go on! I won't interrupt again. I daresay there may be *one*.

DORMOUSE

One, indeed! And so, these three little sisters—they were learning to draw, you know.

ALICE

What did they draw?

DORMOUSE

Treacle.

MAD HATTER

I want a clean cup. Let's all move one place on. (*They do. The* HATTER *is the only one who gets a clean place.* ALICE *is reluctant about moving into the* HARE's *place. But she finally does, looking disapprovingly at the messy remains.*)

ALICE

But I don't understand. Where did they draw the treacle from?

DORMOUSE

You can draw water out of a water well, so I should think you could draw treacle out of a treacle well eh, stupid?

ALICE

But they were *in* the well.

DORMOUSE

Of course they were—*well* in! (ALICE *is too confused for words. The* DORMOUSE *continues, but he's growing sleepy.*) They were learning to draw and they drew all manner of things; everything that begins with an M.

ALICE

Why with an M?

MARCH HARE

Why not? (*Silence. The* DORMOUSE *is dozing off. The* HATTER *pinches him.*)

DORMOUSE (*with a shriek*)

That begins with an M, such as mouse-traps, and the moon, and memory and muchness—you know you say things are much of a muchness—did you ever see such a thing as a drawing of a muchness?

ALICE

Really, now you ask me—I don't think ——

MAD HATTER

Then you shouldn't talk. (*This is more than* ALICE *can bear. She gets up in great disgust.*)

ALICE

I'll never go *there* again! (*The* HARE *and the* HATTER *try to put the* DORMOUSE *into the teapot. BLACK-OUT, as* ALICE *moves into right pinspot.*) It's the stupidest tea party I ever was at in all my life!

SCENE 9

IN THE GARDEN

(† 20, 21, 22 and 23. * 9)

ALICE *finds, when the LIGHTS come up, she is, at last, in the beautiful garden. There is a large rose tree at the left. The roses growing on it are white, but there are three* GARDENERS *at it, busily painting them red. The* GARDENERS *are the Two, Five and Seven of Spades.*)

TWO OF SPADES

Look out now, Five. Don't go splashing paint over me like that.

FIVE OF SPADES

I couldn't help it. Seven jogged my elbow.

SEVEN OF SPADES

That's right, Five. Always lay the blame on others.

FIVE OF SPADES

You'd better not talk. I heard the Queen say only yesterday you deserved to be beheaded.

TWO OF SPADES

What for?

SEVEN OF SPADES

That's none of your business.

FIVE OF SPADES

Yes, it is his business, and I'll tell him. It was for bringing the cook tulip roots instead of onions.

SEVEN OF SPADES

Well, of all the unjust things! (*He catches sight of* ALICE. *They all turn toward her and bow low.*)

ALICE (*curtsying*)

Would you tell me, please, why you are painting those roses? (FIVE *and* SEVEN *look at* TWO.)

TWO OF SPADES

Why, the fact is, you see, Miss, this here ought to have been a *red* rose tree and we put in a white one by mistake, and if the Queen was to find it out, we'd all have our heads cut off, you know. (*Trumpet call from right.*)

FIVE OF SPADES (*pointing off right*)

The Queen! The Queen! (*The* THREE GARDENERS *run, down left, and fall flat upon their faces, as* ALICE *crosses, down right center, and looks off, right, eager to see the* QUEEN. *Another trumpet call ushers in the procession. First,* FOUR CLUBS *cross the stage hurriedly. They are soldiers and wear helmets, and carry spears.* [*See* † 28.] *They stop, extreme left, and turn to face towards* ALICE. *Then* TEN HEARTS *enter, two by two, and take up positions across the background, as in* † 21. *Then follows in solitary splendor the* KNAVE OF HEARTS, *bearing the* KING's *crown on a crimson cushion. He is polite and smiling and half-witted. And last of all in this grand procession come* THE KING *and* QUEEN OF HEARTS. *The* WHITE RABBIT, *a fraction late, and very nervous, passes* ALICE *without noticing her, and finds his place behind the* KNAVE OF HEARTS. *The* QUEEN *stops short in front of* ALICE.)

THE QUEEN OF HEARTS (*pointing at* ALICE, *and addressing the* KNAVE)
Who is this? (THE KNAVE *only bows and smiles in reply. To* KNAVE.) Idiot! (*To* ALICE.) What's your name, child?

ALICE
My name is Alice, so please your Majesty. (*To herself.*) Why, they're only a pack of cards, after all. I needn't be afraid of them!

QUEEN (*indicating the* GARDENERS)
And who are these? (*Their backs being the same as the rest of the pack, she cannot tell whether they are* GARDENERS, SOLDIERS, *or three of her own children.*)

ALICE
How should I know? It's no business of mine. (*She is surprised at her own courage. The* QUEEN *turns crimson with fury, and glares at* ALICE *like a wild beast.*)

QUEEN
Off with her head! Off ——

ALICE (*loudly*)
Nonsense! (*The* QUEEN *is silenced.*)

KING OF HEARTS
Consider, my dear, she is only a child. (*The* QUEEN *considers and turns her attention to the* THREE GARDENERS.)

QUEEN (*to the* KNAVE)

Turn them over! (*The* KNAVE, *still holding the crown, carefully turns the* GARDENERS *over with one foot. To the* GARDENERS.) Get up! (*They do so and begin bowing to the* KING, *the* QUEEN, *and everybody else.*) Leave off that! You make me giddy. (*Turning to the rose tree.*) What *have* you been doing here?

TWO OF HEARTS (*going down on one knee*)

May it please Your Majesty, we were trying ——

QUEEN

I see! Off with their heads! (TWO SOLDIERS *take the* THREE GARDENERS *out. To* ALICE.) Can you play croquet?

ALICE

Yes.

QUEEN

Come on then! (*She starts to march. All mark time in grand processional.* [* 9a.] ALICE *steps along beside the* WHITE RABBIT.)

WHITE RABBIT (*very timidly*)

It's a fine day.

ALICE

Very. Where's the Duchess?

RABBIT

Hush, hush! (*Whispering.*) She is under sentence of execution.

ALICE

What for?

RABBIT

Did you say, " What a pity "?

ALICE

No, I didn't. I don't think it's at all a pity. I said,
" What for? "

RABBIT

She boxed the Queen's ears. (ALICE *bursts into
laughter.*) Oh, hush! The Queen will hear you.
You see, she came rather late, and the Queen
said ——

QUEEN (*stopping procession*)

Get to your places! (*The processional stops, and
then there begins the most curious croquet game that
ALICE has ever seen. The CARDS run about in all directions. The ACE OF HEARTS brings ALICE a flamingo, and makes himself into a wicket, center. ALICE
tucks the body of her flamingo under her arm with its
legs hanging down, but she has great difficulty trying
to hit an imaginary ball through the wicket with its
long wiry neck. Then, too, she finds that she is coming into conflict with the QUEEN who expects to use
the same wicket at the same time, and the game is
made even more difficult by the fact that the wicket
gets up and dances with her. The players all play
at once, quarreling and fighting, until finally the KING
leaves the game and starts to dance with ALICE. When
the QUEEN sees this she is in a furious passion, and*

stamps off right shouting . . .) Off with his head! Off with her head! Off with their heads! (*She exits right, and the* PLAYERS *all go with her, leaving* ALICE *alone with her flamingo. The* DUCHESS *enters from left.*)

DUCHESS

You can't think how glad I am to see you again, you dear old thing. (ALICE *does not answer. She is lost in thought.*) You're thinking about something, my dear, and that makes you forget to talk. I can't tell just now what the moral of that is, but I shall remember it in a bit.

ALICE

Perhaps it hasn't one.

DUCHESS

Tut, tut, child! Everything's got a moral if you can find it. (*The* DUCHESS *rests her chin on* ALICE's *shoulder.* ALICE *makes an effort to be polite.*)

ALICE

The game's going rather better now.

DUCHESS

'Tis so. And the moral of that is, " Oh, 'tis love, 'tis love that makes the world go round."

ALICE

Somebody said that it's done by everybody minding their own business.

DUCHESS

Ah, well! It means much the same thing. And the

moral of that is, " Take care of the sense, and sounds will take care of themselves."

ALICE (*to herself*)
How fond she is of finding morals in things.

DUCHESS
I daresay you're wondering why I don't put my arm around your waist. The reason is that I'm rather doubtful about the temper of your flamingo. Shall I try the experiment?

ALICE (*cautiously*)
It might bite!

DUCHESS
Very true. Flamingoes and mustard both bite. And the moral of that is, " Birds of a feather flock together."

ALICE
But mustard isn't a bird!

DUCHESS
Right as usual. What a clear way you have of putting things!

ALICE
It's a mineral, I think.

DUCHESS
Of course it is. There's a large mustard mine near here. And the moral of that is, " The more there is of mine, the less there is of yours."

ALICE (*who has been thinking, not listening*)

Oh, I know! It's a vegetable. It doesn't look like one but it is.

DUCHESS

I quite agree with you. And the moral of that is, " Be what you would seem to be." Or if you'd like it put more simply, " Never imagine yourself to be otherwise than what it might appear to others that what you were or might have been was not otherwise than what you had been would have appeared to them to be otherwise."

ALICE

I think I should understand that better if I had it written down, but I can't quite follow it as you say it.

DUCHESS (*pleased*)

That's nothing to what I could say if I chose.

ALICE

Pray don't trouble to say it any longer than that. (*The* QUEEN *enters right and steals up behind them.*)

DUCHESS

Oh, don't talk about trouble. I make you a present of everything I've said as yet. And the mora ——— (*Right in the middle of her favorite word she stops, feeling the* QUEEN's *grasp on her shoulder, and turns around, trembling. Weakly.*) A fine day, Your Majesty.

QUEEN (*shouting and stamping*)

Now I give you fair warning, either you or your head must be off, and that in about half no time. Take your choice! (*The* DUCHESS *takes her choice and is gone in a moment, off left. The* QUEEN *is pleased and turns sweetly to* ALICE.) Have you seen the Mock Turtle yet?

ALICE

I don't even know what a Mock Turtle is.

QUEEN

It's the thing Mock Turtle soup is made from.

ALICE

I never saw one nor heard of one.

QUEEN (*taking* ALICE's *flamingo*)

Come on, then, and he shall tell you his history. (*Calls off right.*) Gryphon! (*There is no response.*) Gryphon! (*The* GRYPHON *enters lazily, down right, and sinks to the ground.*) († 24.) Up, lazy thing! and take this young lady to see the Mock Turtle, and to hear his history. (*The* GRYPHON *rises lazily.*) I must go and see after some executions I have ordered. (*She goes off left. BLACKOUT, as* ALICE *and* GRYPHON *cross left to pinspot.*)

GRYPHON (*laughing*)

What fun!

ALICE

What is the fun?

GRYPHON

Why *she!* It's all her fancy, that; they never executes nobody, you know. Come on! (*He crosses right.*)

ALICE

I never was so ordered about in all my life, never! (*She crosses right.*)

SCENE 10

THE MOCK TURTLE

(† 25 and 26.   • 10)

ALICE *joins the* GRYPHON, *right, as LIGHTS come up to reveal the* MOCK TURTLE, *sitting sad and lonely on a little ledge of rock, sighing as if his heart would break.*

ALICE

What is his sorrow?

GRYPHON

It's all his fancy, that; he hasn't got no sorrow, you know. Come on! (*They go up, right center, to the* MOCK TURTLE, *who looks at them with large eyes full of tears, but says nothing.*) This here young lady, she wants for to know your history, she do.

MOCK TURTLE (*in a deep, hollow tone*)

I'll tell it her. Sit down, both of you, and don't speak a word till I've finished. (*They sit down. The* MOCK TURTLE *steps forward off rock, and clears his throat.*) Once—(*sighs*) I was a real turtle. When we were little, we went to school in the sea. (*Brightens as he goes along.*) The master was an old turtle —we used to call him Tortoise.

ALICE

Why did you call him Tortoise if he wasn't one?

MOCK TURTLE

We called him Tortoise because he taught us. (*Angrily.*) Really you are very dull!

GRYPHON

You ought to be ashamed of yourself for asking such a simple question. (*They both look angrily at* ALICE *who feels very small.*) Drive on, old fellow! Don't be all day about it.

MOCK TURTLE

Yes, we went to school in the sea, though you mayn't believe it ——

ALICE

I never said I didn't.

MOCK TURTLE

You did!

GRYPHON

Hold your tongue.

MOCK TURTLE

We had the best of educations. In fact, we went to school every day.

ALICE

I've been to day school, too. You needn't be so proud as all that.

MOCK TURTLE (*anxiously*)

With extras?

ALICE
  Yes, French and Music.

MOCK TURTLE
  And Washing?

ALICE (*indignantly*)
  Certainly not!

MOCK TURTLE
  Ah! Then yours wasn't a really good school. Now
  at *ours* they had at the end of the bill—French,
  Music *and Washing*, extra.

ALICE
  You couldn't have wanted it much, living at the bottom of the sea.

MOCK TURTLE (*sadly*)
  I couldn't afford to learn it. I only took the regular
  course.

ALICE
  What was that?

MOCK TURTLE
  Reeling and Writhing, of course, to begin with. And
  then the different branches of Arithmetic—Ambition,
  Distraction, Uglification and Derision.

ALICE
  I never heard of Uglification. What is it?

GRYPHON (*raising his paws in horror*)
  Never heard of Uglification? You know what to
  beautify is, I suppose?

ALICE

It means to make—anything—prettier.

GRYPHON

Well, then, if you don't know what to uglify is, you *are* a simpleton.

ALICE (*hastily*)

And how many hours a day did you do lessons?

MOCK TURTLE

Ten hours the first day, nine the next, and so on.

ALICE

What a curious plan!

GRYPHON

That's the reason they are called lessons. Because they lessen from day to day.

ALICE (*thoughtfully*)

Then the eleventh day must have been a holiday.

MOCK TURTLE

Of course it was.

ALICE

But how did you manage on the twelfth?

GRYPHON (*decidedly*)

That's enough about lessons. Tell her something about the games now. (*The* MOCK TURTLE *tries to speak but is choked with sobs. The* GRYPHON *slaps him on the back. To* ALICE.) Same as if he had a bone in his throat.

MOCK TURTLE (*to* GRYPHON)

Thank you.   (*To* ALICE.)   You may not have lived much under the sea.

ALICE

I haven't.

MOCK TURTLE

And perhaps you were never introduced to a Lobster.

ALICE

I once tasted —— No, never!

MOCK TURTLE

So you have no idea what a delightful thing a Lobster Quadrille is

ALICE

No, indeed.   What sort of a dance is it?

MOCK TURTLE

Would you like to see a little of it?

ALICE

Very much indeed.

MOCK TURTLE (*to the* GRYPHON)

Come, let's try the first figure.   We can do it without the lobsters, you know.   (*Hopefully.*)   Which shall sing?

GRYPHON

Oh, you sing.   I've forgotten the words.   (*So the* MOCK TURTLE, *pleased, begins solemnly to sing, as he and the* GRYPHON *dance up and down, minuet fashion, until the chorus, when the* GRYPHON, *taking* ALICE *as*

*a partner, whirls her around and around so fast that
she is very glad when it is over at last.*)

MOCK TURTLE

" Will you walk a little faster!" said a whiting to a
snail.

" There's a porpoise close behind us, and he's treading
on my tail.

See how eagerly the lobsters and the turtles all ad-
vance!

They are waiting on the shingle—will you come and
join the dance?

Will you, won't you, will you, won't you, will you join
the dance?

Will you, won't you, will you, won't you, will you join
the dance?

" You can really have no notion how delightful it will
be

When they take us up and throw us, with the lobsters,
out to sea!"

The further off from England the nearer 'tis to
France,

Then turn not pale, beloved snail, but come and join
the dance.

Will you, won't you, will you, won't you, will you join
the dance?

Will you, won't you, will you, won't you, won't you
join the dance?

ALICE

Thank you. It's a very interesting dance to watch.

And I do so like that curious song about the whiting.

MOCK TURTLE
Oh, as to the whiting, they —— You've seen them, of course?

ALICE.   Yes, I've often seen them at dinn —— (*She checks herself just in time.*)

MOCK TURTLE
I don't know where Dinn may be, but if you've seen them so often, of course you know what they look like. (*He yawns and shuts his eyes.*)

GRYPHON
Do you know why it's called a whiting?

ALICE
I never thought about it.   Why?

GRYPHON (*solemnly*)
It does the boots and shoes.

ALICE
Does the boots and shoes?

GRYPHON
Why, what are your shoes done with?

ALICE
With blacking, I believe.

GRYPHON (*impressively*)
Boots and shoes under the sea are done with whiting. Now you know.

ALICE

And what are they made of?

GRYPHON

Soles and eels, of course. Any shrimp could have told you that.

ALICE

If I'd been the whiting in the song, I'd have said to the porpoise, " Keep back, please, we don't want you with us."

MOCK TURTLE (*waking up quite as suddenly as he went to sleep*)

They were obliged to have him. No wise fish would go anywhere without a porpoise.

ALICE

Wouldn't it really?

MOCK TURTLE

Of course not. Why, if a fish came to me and told me he was going on a journey, I'd say, " With what porpoise? "

ALICE

Don't you mean purpose?

MOCK TURTLE

I mean what I say.

GRYPHON

Shall we try another figure of the Lobster Quadrille? Or would you like the Mock Turtle to sing you a song?

ALICE

Oh, a song, please, if the Mock Turtle would be so kind.

GRYPHON (*offended*)

H'm, no accounting for tastes. Sing her Turtle Soup, will you, old fellow? (* *10a.*)

MOCK TURTLE

Beautiful Soup so rich and green,
Waiting in a hot tureen!
Who for such dainties would not stoop?
Soup of the evening, beautiful soup!

Soup of the evening, beautiful soup!
Soup of the evening, beautiful soup!
Beau-ootiful soo-oop!
Beau-ootiful soo-oop!
Soo-oop of the e-e-e-evening,
Beautiful, beautiful soup!

Beautiful Soup! Who cares for fish,
Game, or any other dish?
Who would give all else for two p
ennyworth only of beautiful soup?

Soup of the evening, beautiful soup!
Soup of the evening, beautiful soup!
Beau-ootiful soo-oop!
Beau-ootiful soo-oop!
Soo-oop of the e-e-e-evening,
Beautiful, beautiful soup!

(*The* WHITE RABBIT, *dressed as Herald* [† 27], *dashes across from right to left.*)

THE WHITE RABBIT

The trial's beginning! The trial's beginning! The trial's beginning! (*He exits, left. BLACKOUT. The* GRYPHON *takes* ALICE *by the hand, and leads her to pinspot, right.*)

GRYPHON

Come on!

ALICE

What trial is it?

GRYPHON

Come on!

SCENE 11

THE TRIAL

(† 28, 29, 30, 31 and 32. • 11)

ALICE *finds, when the LIGHTS come up, that she and the* GRYPHON *are standing at the extreme right in the courtroom of the* KING *and* QUEEN OF HEARTS, *who are seated on their throne, up center, with a great crowd of* BIRDS, BEASTS, *and* CARDS *assembled about them. In the jury box to the left of the throne sit the* DUCK, *the* DORMOUSE, *and the* FROG *and* FISH FOOTMEN. *In the spectators' bench to the right sit the* DUCHESS *and her* COOK. *The* KNAVE *stands in chains, down right center, and, in the very middle of the courtroom, there is a table with a large dish of tarts upon it. At the table sit the* GOAT, *the* MOUSE, *the* LORY, *and the* EAGLET, *dressed in white wigs, as clerks. Flanking the courtroom are the* CLUBS *and* HEARTS. *The* WHITE RABBIT, *in his Herald costume, stands right of* KING, *bearing a trumpet and a scroll.* ALICE *spies the tarts at once.*

ALICE

Oooh! What lovely tarts. I wish they'd get the trial done and hand round the refreshments.

EVERYBODY

Shush!

ALICE (*moving center. In a loud whisper*)

That's the Judge because of his great wig. And that's the jury-box. And I suppose those creatures are the jurors. What are they doing? They can't have anything to put down yet before the trial's begun.

GRYPHON (*whispering*)

They're putting down their names for fear they should forget them before the end of the trial.

ALICE (*aloud*)

Stupid things!

WHITE RABBIT

Silence in the court! (*The* KING *puts on his spectacles and looks at* ALICE.)

KING

Young lady, just look along the road and tell me whom you see. (ALICE *looks off, left.*)

ALICE

I see nobody on the road.

KING

I only wish I had such eyes! To be able to see nobody, and at that distance, too! Why, it's as much as I can do to see real people by this light!

ALICE

I see somebody now. But he comes very slowly, and what curious attitudes he goes into!

KING

Not at all. He's an Anglo-Saxon messenger, and those are Anglo-Saxon attitudes. He only does them when he's happy. His name is Haigha. (*Pronounced to rhyme with Mayor.*)

ALICE

I love my love with an H, because he is Happy. I hate him with an H because he is Hideous. I feed him with Ham-sandwiches, and Hay. His name is Haigha and he lives ——

KING (*in a matter-of-fact tone*)

He lives on the Hill. The other messenger is called Hatta. I must have two, you know, one to come, and one to go.

ALICE

I beg your pardon?

KING

It isn't respectable to beg. (*The* MARCH HARE *enters, skipping up and down, wiggling like an eel, with his*

*loosely gloved paws waving like fans on his either
side. He wears a bag hanging on a string around
his neck.* [*See* † 29.] *He is too out of breath to
speak and stands in middle of floor making wild ges-
ticulations at the* KING. *Trying to take his poor
messenger's mind off himself.*) This young lady loves
you with an H. (*The* HARE *dashes to the foot of
the throne.*) You alarm me! I feel faint! Give me
a ham sandwich! (*The* HARE *reaches in his bag and
pulls out a small sandwich which the* KING *devours
greedily.*) Another!

MARCH HARE (*peeking in his bag*)
    There's nothing left but hay now.

KING (*faintly*)
    Hay, then! (*The* HARE *gives him some hay which he
    munches happily. With his mouth full.*) There's
    nothing like eating hay when you're faint.

ALICE
    I should think throwing cold water over you would be
    better.

KING (*quite revived*)
    I didn't say there was nothing *better*. I said there
    was nothing *like* it. (*He pauses for that to penetrate.
    To the* HARE.) Who did you pass on the road?

MARCH HARE
    Nobody.

KING
    Quite right. This young lady saw him, too. So, of
    course, nobody walks slower than you. Now that

you've got your breath, you may tell us what they're
saying in the town.

MARCH HARE

I'll whisper it. (*He tiptoes up to* KING *and prepares
to whisper through his hands in the* KING'*s ear, then
shouts.*) The trial ought to begin!!!! (*The* KING
jumps violently.)

KING

Do you call that a whisper? If you do such a thing
again, I'll have you buttered. It went through and
through my head like an earthquake! Sit down!
(HARE *seats himself among spectators.*) Herald,
read the accusation. (WHITE RABBIT *blows three
blasts on his trumpet, unrolls the parchment scroll
and reads.*)

WHITE RABBIT

" The Queen of Hearts, she made some tarts,
    All on a summer day:
    The Knave of Hearts, he stole those tarts,
    And took them quite away! "

KING (*to the jury*)

Consider your verdict!

WHITE RABBIT

Not yet, not yet! There's a great deal more to come
before that.

KING (*clearing his throat*)

Call the first witness!

WHITE RABBIT (*first blowing his trumpet*)

First witness! (*Enter the* HATTER, *left. He holds a teacup in one hand and a piece of bread and butter in the other.*) († *30.*)

MAD HATTER

I beg pardon, Majesty, for bringing these in: but I hadn't quite finished my tea when I was sent for.

KING

You ought to have finished. When did you begin?

MAD HATTER

Fourteenth of March, I think it was.

MARCH HARE

Fifteenth.

DORMOUSE

Sixteenth.

KING (*to* JURY)

Write that down. (*There is a great flourish of pencils. To the* HATTER.) Take off your hat.

MAD HATTER

It isn't mine.

KING

Stolen! (*He turns to* JURY *who gasp and make a memorandum.*)

MAD HATTER

I keep them to sell. I've none of my own. I'm a hatter. (*The* QUEEN *puts on her spectacles and begins to stare hard at the* HATTER, *who grows fidgety.*)

KING

Give your evidence.   And don't be nervous or I'll have
you executed on the spot.   (*The* HATTER *becomes so
confused he bites a large piece out of his teacup, instead of his bread and butter*.)

QUEEN (*to* OFFICER OF THE COURT.)

Bring me the list of the singers in the last concert!
(*At this the* HATTER *trembles so hard he shakes both
his shoes off*.)   († *30*.)

KING

Give your evidence or I'll have you executed whether
you're nervous or not.

MAD HATTER (*in a trembly voice*)

I'm a poor man, Your Majesty, and I hadn't but just
begun my tea, not above a week or so ago, and what
with the bread and butter getting so thin, and the
twinkling of the tea ——

KING

The twinkling of *what?*

MAD HATTER

It began with the tea.

KING

Of course twinkling begins with a T.   Do you take
me for a dunce?   If that's all you know, you may
stand down.

MAD HATTER

I can't go no lower.   I'm on the floor as it is.

KING

Then you may *sit* down.

MAD HATTER

I'd rather finish my tea.

KING

You may go! (*The* MAD HATTER *runs off, left.*) († *31*.)

QUEEN

Just take his head off outside!

KING (*to the* JURY)

Consider your verdict! (*During the excitement, the* KNAVE *has dropped a paper, which a* SOLDIER *delivers to the* WHITE RABBIT.)

THE WHITE RABBIT

There's more evidence to come yet, please Your Majesty. This paper has just been picked up. It's a set of verses.

QUEEN

Are they in the prisoner's handwriting?

THE WHITE RABBIT

No, they're not. And that's the queerest thing about it. (JURY *all look puzzled.*)

KING

He must have imitated someone else's hand. (JURY *much relieved.*)

KNAVE

Please, Your Majesty, I didn't write it, and they

can't prove I did.   There's no name signed at the end.

KING (*cleverly*)
   If you didn't sign it, that only makes matters worse.
   You *must* have meant some mischief or you'd have
   signed your name like an honest man.   (*There is a
   general clapping of hands at this.*)

QUEEN
   That proves his guilt.

ALICE
   It proves nothing of the sort!   Why, you don't even
   know what they're about!

KING (*to the* RABBIT)
   Read them!

THE WHITE RABBIT
   Where shall I begin, please Your Majesty?

KING (*gravely*)
   Begin at the beginning and go on till you come to the
   end; then stop!

THE WHITE RABBIT
   　　" They told me you had been to her,
   　　　　And mentioned me to him;
   　　　She gave me a good character,
   　　　　But said I could not swim.

   　　" He sent them word I had not gone
   　　　　(We know it to be true) :
   　　　If she should push the matter on,
   　　　　What would become of you?

" I gave her one, they gave him two,
    You gave us three or more;
  They all returned from him to you,
    Though they were mine, before.

" I gave her one, they gave him two,
    You gave us three or more;
  They all returned from him to you,
    Though they were mine, before.

" If I or she should chance to be
    Involved in this affair,
  He trusts to you to set them free,
    Exactly as we were.
  He trusts to you to set them free,
    Exactly as we were.

" My notion was that you had been
    (Before she had this fit)
  An obstacle that came between
    Him and ourselves, and it.
  An obstacle that came between
    Him and ourselves, and it.

" Don't let him know she liked them best,
    For this must ever be
  A secret, kept from all the rest,
    Between yourself and me.
  A secret, kept from all the rest,
    Between yourself and me."

KING (*rubbing his hands*)
That's the most important piece of evidence we've heard yet. So now let the jury ——

ALICE (*moving center*)

If any of them can explain it, I'll give him sixpence. *I* don't believe there's an atom of meaning in it.

JURY (*softly and simultaneously, while writing out the syllables on their slates*)

She—does-n't be-lieve there's an a-tom of mean-ing in it.

KING

If there's no meaning in it, that saves a world of trouble, you know, as we needn't try to find any. And yet, I don't know—(*he examines the paper through large binoculars, handed to him by the* WHITE RABBIT, *down whose back they have been hanging.*) I seem to see some meaning in them, after all. "—I said I could not swim ——" You can't swim, can you?

KNAVE (*sadly*)

Do I look like it?

KING

All right so far. "We know it to be true"—that's the jury, of course—"I gave her one, they gave him two"—why, that must be what he did with the tarts, you know.

ALICE

But it goes on, "They all returned from him to you."

KING

Why, there they are! (*Triumphantly.*) Nothing can be clearer than that. Then again—"Before she had this fit ——" You never had fits, my dear, I think?

QUEEN (*furiously*)

Never!

KING

Then the words don't *fit* you! (*He beams. Dead silence. Angrily.*) It's a pun! (*All laugh.*)

ALICE (*rising*)

It's a lie!

KING

What do you know about this business?

ALICE

Nothing.

KING

Nothing *whatever?*

ALICE

Nothing whatever.

KING

That's very important. (*He turns to the* JURY, *who, as usual, make a great business of writing it down.*)

THE WHITE RABBIT (*respectfully*)

*Un*important, Your Majesty, means of course.

KING

*Un*important, of course, I meant. (*To himself.*) Important, unimportant, important, unimportant, imp, ump. (*Aloud.*) Unimportant! Yes, yes, to be sure. (*To* JURY.) Consider your verdict!

QUEEN

No, no! Sentence first; verdict afterwards.

ALICE

Stuff and nonsense! The idea of having the sentence first.

QUEEN (*in a rage*)

Hold your tongue! (*The* CARDS, HEARTS *and* CLUBS *start to close in on her from both sides.*)

ALICE

I won't!

QUEEN (*at the top of her voice*)

Off with her head!

ALL (*reaching up*)

Off with her head!!! (CARDS *move closer.*)

ALICE. Who cares for you! You're nothing but a pack of cards! (*BLACKOUT with lantern effect.* [† 33. * 11a.] *The* WHOLE PACK OF CARDS *rises up in the air, and comes flying down upon her. She tries to beat them off, then turns right and runs* [*in place*] *as fast as she can go.*) (* 11b.)

CURTAIN

ACT TWO

SCENE 1

The Red Queen

(† 34, 35, and 36. • 12)

At rise, ALICE *is seen still running, but now she is facing left. She slows down wearily and comes to a stop. As LIGHTS come up, she finds herself in a land that is marked out in squares, like a huge chessboard, with a large tree at the right. Presently, from the left, with a thump, thump of footsteps, the* RED QUEEN *enters and comes face to face with* ALICE.

RED QUEEN

Where do you come from and where are you going? Look up, speak nicely, and don't twiddle your fingers.

ALICE (*attending to all these directions as well as she can*)

You see I've lost my way.

RED QUEEN

I don't know what you mean by *your* way, all the ways about here belong to *me*—but why did you come out here at all? Curtsey while you're thinking what to say. It saves time.

ALICE (*aside*)

I'll try it when I go home, the next time I'm a little late for dinner.

RED QUEEN (*looking at her watch*)

It's time for you to answer now. Open your mouth a *little* wider when you speak and always say " Your Majesty."

ALICE

I only wanted to see what the garden was like, Your Majesty ——

RED QUEEN (*patting* ALICE *on the head which she doesn't like at all*)

That's right, though when you say " garden "—*I've* seen gardens, compared with which this would be a wilderness.

ALICE (*going right on*)

—and I thought I'd try and find my way to the top of that hill.

RED QUEEN

When you you say " hill "—*I* could show you hills, in comparison with which you'd call that a valley.

ALICE

No, I shouldn't, a hill *can't* be a valley, you know. That would be nonsense ——

RED QUEEN

You may call it " nonsense " if you like, but *I've* heard nonsense, compared with which that would be as sensible as a dictionary! (ALICE *curtsies again as she is afraid by the* QUEEN's *tone that she is a little offended.*)

ALICE (*surveying the view*)

I declare it's marked out just like a large chessboard. It's a great huge game of chess that's being played— all over the world—if this *is* the world at all, you know. Oh, what fun it is! How I *wish* I was part of it. I wouldn't mind being a Pawn, if only I might join—though of course I should *like* to be a Queen best. (*She glances shyly at the* QUEEN, *who smiles pleasantly*.)

RED QUEEN

That's easily managed. You can be the White Queen's Pawn, if you like, as Lily's too young to play; and you're in the Second Square to begin with: when you get to the Eighth Square, you'll be a Queen. (*They begin to run hand in hand—the scene does not change —the* QUEEN *runs so fast* ALICE *can scarcely keep up with her and still the* QUEEN *keeps crying:*) Faster, faster!

ALICE (*to herself*)

I wonder if all the things move along with us?

RED QUEEN. Faster! Don't try to talk! (ALICE *falters and falls back a little*.) Faster! Faster!

ALICE (*at last getting her breath*)

Are we nearly there?

RED QUEEN

Nearly there! Why, we passed it ten minutes ago! Faster! (*They run on in silence for a while*.) Now! Now! Faster! Faster! (*The* QUEEN *pulls* ALICE *up*

*in line with herself again. They run on . . . then
slowly come to a stop.* ALICE *drops to ground. The*
QUEEN *seats* ALICE *under the tree. Kindly.*) You
may rest a little now.

ALICE (*looking around in surprise*)

Why, I do believe we've been under this tree the whole
time! Everything's just as it was!

RED QUEEN

Of course it is. What would you have it?

ALICE

Well, in *our* country, you'd generally get to somewhere else—if you ran very fast for a long time as
we've been doing.

RED QUEEN

A slow sort of country! Now, *here*, you see, it takes
all the running *you* can do to keep in the same place.
If you want to get somewhere else, you must run at
least twice as fast as that!

ALICE

I'd rather not try, please! I'm quite content to stay
here—only I *am* so hot and thirsty!

RED QUEEN

I know what *you'd* like. (*Takes a large, hard-water
biscuit out of her pocket.*) Have a biscuit? (ALICE
*takes it but finds it very dry. She chokes and puts
remainder of biscuit in her pocket.*) While you're re-
freshing yourself, I'll just take the measurements.
(*She marches to a point downstage, right, in front of
the tree, where she begins to measure with a tape*

measure, taking little sidesteps from right to left, and marking the end of each " square " with a bounce in her knees, and a gesture of her hand, as though placing a peg.) At the end of two yards . . . *(she takes two sidesteps left. Bounce)* I shall give you your directions. Have another biscuit?

ALICE

No, thank you, one's *quite* enough.

RED QUEEN

Thirst quenched, I hope? At the end of *three* yards . . . *(business)* I shall repeat them for fear of your forgetting them. At the end of *four* . . . *(business)* I shall say good-bye. And at the end of *five* . . . *(business)* I shall go! *(She marches back to her starting point and begins walking slowly along the line that she has measured, describing each square with suitable gesture.)* A pawn goes two squares in its first move, you know. So you'll go *very* quickly through the Third Square . . . by railway, I should think . . . and you'll find yourself in the Fourth Square in no time. Well, *that* square belongs to Tweedledum and Tweedledee . . . the Fifth is mostly water . . . the Sixth belongs to Humpty Dumpty. . . . But you make no remark?

ALICE

I . . . I didn't know I had to make one just then.

RED QUEEN

You *should* have said, " It's extremely kind of you to tell me all this," . . . however, we'll suppose it said

. . . the Seventh Square is all forest . . . however,
one of the Knights will show you the way . . . and in
the Eighth Square we shall be Queens together, and
it's all feasting and fun! (*She turns to* ALICE. ALICE
gets up and curtsies.)   Speak in French when you
can't think of the English for a thing.   Turn out
your toes when you walk, and remember who you are!
(*She turns left and starts running.*)

ALICE

She *can* run very fast!

RED QUEEN

Good-bye. (*She exits, left.   BLACKOUT.   Shrill
whistle of steam engine.*)

SCENE 2

THE RAILWAY CARRIAGE

(† 37.   * 13)

LIGHTS up. ALICE *finds herself, dressed for travel,
riding in a railway carriage.   Her only visible com-
panions are a* GENTLEMAN DRESSED IN WHITE PAPER,
and a GOAT. *But the air is filled with* VOICES. *The*
GUARD *is putting his head in the window.*

GUARD

Tickets, please!   Now then!   Show your ticket, child!

GENTLEMAN DRESSED IN WHITE PAPER

Don't keep him waiting, child!   Why, his time . . .

VOICES

   . . . is worth a thousand pounds a minute!

ALICE

   I'm afraid I haven't got one; there wasn't a ticket-office where I came from.

GENTLE VOICE

   There wasn't room for one where she came from.   The land there . . .

VOICES

   . . . is worth a thousand pounds an inch!

GUARD

   Don't make excuses: you should have bought one from the engine driver.

ANOTHER VOICE

   The man that drives the engine.   Why, the smoke alone . . .

VOICES

   . . . is worth a thousand pounds a puff!

ALICE

   Then there's no use in speaking.

BEETLE'S VOICE

   Better say nothing at all.   Language . . .

VOICES

   . . . is worth a thousand pounds a word!

ALICE

   I shall dream about a thousand pounds tonight, I

know I shall! (*All this while the* GUARD *is looking at her, first through a telescope, then an opera glass, then a reading glass.*)

GUARD

You're traveling the wrong way. (*He exits left.*)

GENTLEMAN DRESSED IN WHITE PAPER

So young a child ought to know which way she's going, even if she doesn't know her own name!

GOAT

She ought to know her way to the ticket office, even if she doesn't know her alphabet.

BEETLE'S VOICE

She'll have to go back from here as luggage!

HOARSE VOICE

Change engines. (*Shrill scream of* TRAIN WHISTLE. ALICE *jumps up in alarm.*)

GENTLEMAN DRESSED IN WHITE PAPER

It's only a brook we have to jump over.

ALICE

However, it'll take us into the Fourth Square, that's some comfort. (*BLACKOUT.*)

SCENE 3

TWEEDLEDUM AND TWEEDLEDEE

(† 38, 39, 40 and 41. ＊ 14)

LIGHTS up. ALICE *finds herself in the presence of* TWO FAT LITTLE MEN. *They are standing under a tree, each with an arm about the other's neck. One of them has* " DUM " *embroidered on his collar, and the other* " DEE."

ALICE

I suppose they've each got Tweedle round at the back of the collar. (*She starts around to see.*)

TWEEDLEDUM

If you think we're wax-works, you ought to pay, you know. Wax-works aren't made to be looked at for nothing—nohow!

TWEEDLEDEE

Contrariwise. If you think we're alive, you ought to speak.

ALICE

I'm sure I'm very sorry.

TWEEDLEDUM

I know what you're thinking about, but it isn't so, nohow.

TWEEDLEDEE

Contrariwise. If it was so, it might be; and if it were so, it would be, but as it isn't, it ain't. That's logic.

ALICE

I was thinking which is the best way out of this wood. It's getting dark. Would you tell me, please? (TWEE-DLEDUM *and* TWEEDLEDEE *only look at each other and grin.*) They look so exactly like a couple of school-boys! (*She points at* TWEEDLEDUM, *like a school teacher.*) First boy!

TWEEDLEDUM

Nohow.

ALICE

Next boy!

TWEEDLEDEE

Contrariwise.

ALICE

Would you tell me, please . . .

TWEEDLEDEE

You like poetry?

ALICE

Ye-es, pretty well . . . some poetry . . .

TWEEDLEDEE

What shall we repeat to her?

TWEEDLEDUM (*hugging his brother affectionately*)
" The Walrus and the Carpenter." That's longest.

ALICE

If it's very long, would you tell me, please, which road . . . (TWEEDLEDUM *and* TWEEDLEDEE *move down left in neat glides, still with their arms around*

each other's necks, and take position for song.
[* *14a.*] ALICE *sits, down right.*)

TWEEDLEDUM

> The sun was shining on the sea,

TWEEDLEDEE

> Shining with all his might:

TWEEDLEDUM

> He did his very best to make

TWEEDLEDEE

> The billows smooth and bright . . .

TWEEDLEDUM

> And this was odd,

TWEEDLEDEE

> Because it was

TWEEDLEDUM and **TWEEDLEDEE**

> The middle of the night.

TWEEDLEDEE

> The Walrus and the Carpenter
> Were walking close at hand;
> They wept like anything to see
> Such quantities of sand:

TWEEDLEDUM

> " If this were only cleared away,"

TWEEDLEDEE

> They said,

TWEEDLEDUM and TWEEDLEDEE
"It would be grand!"

TWEEDLEDUM
"O, Oysters, come and walk with us!"
The Walrus did beseech.
"A pleasant walk, a pleasant talk,
Along the briny beach;

TWEEDLEDEE
We cannot do with more than four,
To give a hand to each."

The eldest oyster looked at him,
But never a word he said:
The eldest oyster winked his eye,
And shook his heavy head . . .
Meaning to say he did not choose
To leave the oyster bed.

TWEEDLEDUM
But four young oysters hurried up,
All eager for the treat:
Their coats were brushed, their faces washed;
Their shoes were clean and neat . . .
And this was odd, because, you know,
They hadn't any feet.

Four other oysters followed them,
And yet another four;
And thick and fast they came at last,
And more, and more, and more . . .

All hopping through the frothy waves,
And scrambling to the shore.

TWEEDLEDEE

The Walrus and the Carpenter
Walked on a mile or so,
And then they rested on a rock
Conveniently low:
And all the little oysters stood
And waited in a row.

" The time has come," the Walrus said,
" To talk of many things;
Of shoes . . . and ships . . . and sealing-wax . . .
Of cabbages . . . and kings . . .

TWEEDLEDUM

And why the sea is boiling hot . . .
And whether pigs have wings.

TWEEDLEDEE

A loaf of bread," the Walrus said,
Is what we chiefly need:

TWEEDLEDUM

Pepper and vinegar besides
Are very good indeed. . . .

TWEEDLEDUM and TWEEDLEDEE

Now if you're ready, Oysters dear,
We can begin to feed."

TWEEDLEDUM

" But not on us!" the Oysters cried,

Turning a little blue.
" After such kindness, that would be
A dismal thing to do! "

TWEEDLEDEE

" The night is fine," the Walrus said,
" Do you admire the view? "

TWEEDLEDUM

" It seems a shame," the Walrus said,
" To play them such a trick,
After we've brought them out so far,
And made them trot so quick! "

TWEEDLEDEE

The Carpenter said nothing but
" The butter's spread too thick! "

" I weep for you," the Walrus said,
" I deeply sympathize."

TWEEDLEDUM

With sobs and tears he sorted out
Those of the largest size,
Holding his pocket-handkerchief
Before his streaming eyes.

TWEEDLEDUM and **TWEEDLEDEE**

" O, Oysters," said the Carpenter,
" You've had a pleasant run!
Shall we be trotting home again? "

TWEEDLEDEE

But answer came there none . . .

TWEEDLEDUM

But answer came there none . . .

TWEEDLEDUM and TWEEDLEDEE

And this was scarcely odd, because
They'd eaten every one.

(TWEEDLEDUM *and* TWEEDLEDEE *return, with neat glides center, and* ALICE *rises to join them.*) (* *14b.*)

ALICE

I like the Walrus best, because you see he was a *little* sorry for the poor oysters.

TWEEDLEDEE

He ate more than the Carpenter though. You see he held his handkerchief in front so that the Carpenter couldn't count how many he took: contrariwise.

ALICE

That was mean! Then I like the Carpenter best . . . if he didn't eat so many as the Walrus.

TWEEDLEDUM

But he ate as many as he could get.

ALICE

Well! They were *both* very unpleasant characters. At any rate I'd better be getting out of this wood, for really it's coming on very dark. Do you think it's going to rain? (TWEEDLEDEE *picks up an enormous umbrella that lies behind him on the floor.*)

TWEEDLEDEE

No, I don't think it is: at least not under *here*. Nohow.

ALICE

But it may rain outside?

TWEEDLEDEE

It may if it chooses: we've no objection. Contrariwise. (*They exit right.*)

ALICE

Selfish things!

SCENE 4

THE WHITE QUEEN

(† 42. * 15)

A shawl is blown in by the wind from left. (* *15a.*)

ALICE

Here's somebody's shawl being blown off. I'm glad I
happened to be in the way. (*The* WHITE QUEEN *is
blown in.* [* *15b.*] *Helpless, frightened, with her
arms outstretched wildly, she goes from left to right,
and back, left again, where she finally settles repeat-
ing in a whisper to herself:*)

WHITE QUEEN

Bread-and-butter, bread-and-butter, bread-and-butter.

ALICE (*timidly*)

Am I addressing the White Queen?

WHITE QUEEN

Well, yes, if you call that a-dressing. It isn't my nur-
tion of the thing at all.

ALICE

If Your Majesty will only tell me the right way to
begin, I'll do it as well as I can.

WHITE QUEEN (*with a groan*)

But I don't want it done at all. I've been a-dressing
myself for the last two hours.

ALICE (*aside*)

Every single thing's crooked and she is all over pins.
(*To the* WHITE QUEEN.)   May I put your shawl
straight for you?

WHITE QUEEN (*in a melancholy voice*)

I don't know what's the matter with it.   It's out of
temper, I think.   I've pinned it here and I've pinned
it there, but there's no pleasing it!

ALICE

It *can't* go straight, you know, if you pin it all on
one side, and dear me, what a state your hair is in.

WHITE QUEEN (*with a sigh*)

The brush has got entangled in it and I lost the comb
yesterday.

ALICE (*carefully releasing the brush and altering some
of the pins*)

Come, you look rather better now, but really you
should have a lady's maid.

WHITE QUEEN

I am sure I'll take *you* with pleasure! Twopence a week and jam every other day.

ALICE (*laughing*)

I don't want you to hire *me*—and I don't care for jam.

WHITE QUEEN

It's very good jam.

ALICE

Well, I don't want any *today* at any rate.

WHITE QUEEN

You couldn't have it if you *did* want it. The rule is jam tomorrow and jam yesterday but never jam *today*.

ALICE

It must come sometimes to " Jam today."

WHITE QUEEN

No, it can't; it's jam every *other* day; today isn't any other day, you know.

ALICE

I don't understand you. It is dreadfully confusing.

WHITE QUEEN

That's the effect of living backwards, it always makes one a little giddy at first ——

ALICE

Living backwards! I never heard of such a thing

WHITE QUEEN

But there is one great advantage in it, that one's memory works both ways.

ALICE

I'm sure *mine* only works one way. I can't remember things before they happen.

WHITE QUEEN (*shortly*)

It's a poor sort of memory that only works backwards.

ALICE

What sort of things do *you* remember best?

WHITE QUEEN (*carelessly*)

Oh, things that happened the week after next   For instance now (*she sticks a large piece of sticking plaster on her finger*) there's the King's Messenger. He's in prison now, being punished: and the trial doesn't even begin till next Wednesday: and of course the crime comes last of all.

ALICE

Suppose he never commits the crime?

WHITE QUEEN

That would be all the better, wouldn't it? (*She binds the plaster round her finger with a bit of ribbon.*)

ALICE

Of course it would be all the better, but it wouldn't be all the better his being punished.

WHITE QUEEN

You're wrong *there*, at any rate! Were *you* ever punished?

ALICE

Only for faults.

WHITE QUEEN (*triumphantly*)

And you were all the better for it, I know!

ALICE

Yes, but then I *had* done the things I was punished for: that makes all the difference.

WHITE QUEEN

But if you *hadn't* done them, that would have been better still; better and better and better! (*Her voice rises higher at each " better " till at last it is a squeak, as she flies to stage right.*)

ALICE

There's a mistake somewhere ——

WHITE QUEEN (*screaming like a steam whistle and shaking her hand about as if she wanted to shake it off*)

Oh, oh, oh! My finger's bleeding. Oh, oh, oh, oh!

ALICE (*holding her hands over her ears*)

What *is* the matter? Have you pricked your finger?

WHITE QUEEN

I haven't pricked it *yet*, but I soon shall. Oh, oh, oh!

ALICE (*trying not to laugh*)

When do you expect to do it?

WHITE QUEEN (*groaning*)

When I fasten my shawl again; the brooch will come undone directly. Oh, oh! (*At these words the brooch flies open and* WHITE QUEEN *clutches wildly at it and tries to clasp it again.*)

ALICE

Take care! You're holding it all crooked! (*She catches at the brooch, but too late. The pin has slipped and the* WHITE QUEEN *has pricked her finger.*)

WHITE QUEEN (*with a smile*)

There, you see! That accounts for the bleeding! Now you understand the way things happen here.

ALICE

But why don't you scream *now?*

WHITE QUEEN

Why, I've done all the screaming already. What would be the good of having it all over again?

ALICE

I'm glad it's getting lighter. I thought it was the night coming on.

WHITE QUEEN

I wish I could manage to be glad! Only I never can remember the rule. You must be very happy, living in this wood, and being glad whenever you like!

ALICE (*in a melancholy voice—two large tears rolling down her cheeks*)

Only it's so *very* lonely here!

WHITE QUEEN (*wringing her hands in despair*)

Oh, don't go on like that! Consider what a great girl you are. Consider what a long way you've come today. Consider what o'clock it is. Consider anything only don't cry!

ALICE (*laughing through her tears*)
Can *you* keep from crying by considering things?

WHITE QUEEN (*with great decision*)
That's the way it's done; nobody can do two things at once, you know. Let's consider your age to begin with—how old are you?

ALICE
I am seven and a half exactly.

WHITE QUEEN
You needn't say " exactually." I can believe it without that. Now I'll give *you* something to believe. I'm just one hundred and one, five months and a day.

ALICE
I can't believe *that!*

WHITE QUEEN (*in a pitying tone*)
Can't you? Try again! Draw a long breath and shut your eyes.

ALICE (*laughing*)
There's no use trying. One can't believe impossible things.

WHITE QUEEN
I daresay you haven't had much practise. When I was your age, I always did it for half an hour a day.

Why, sometimes, I've believed as many as six impossible things before breakfast. There goes the shawl again! (*She seizes shawl. Triumphantly.*) I've got it! Now you shall see me pin it on again, all by myself!

ALICE

Then I hope your finger is better now?

WHITE QUEEN

Oh, much better. Much be-etter! Be-etter! Be-e-e-etter! Be-e-ehh! (*She flies off, right. DIM-OUT.*)

SCENE 5

THE SHEEP SHOP

(† 43.   * 16)

The bleating continues loud and insistent, and when the LIGHTS come up, ALICE finds that she is in a shop, leaning her elbows on the counter and looking across at an old SHEEP, who is sitting in an armchair, knitting, and looking at her every now and then through a great pair of spectacles.

SHEEP (*in a bleating voice*)
What is it you want to buy?

ALICE

I don't quite know yet. I should like to look all around me first, if I might.

SHEEP

You may look in front of you, and on both sides, if
you like; but you can't look all round you, unless
you've got eyes in the back of your head. (ALICE
turns round and round, looking from shelf to shelf.)

ALICE (*in a plaintive tone*)
Things flow about so here.

SHEEP

Are you a child or a teetotum? (*She picks up more
needles.*) You'll make me giddy soon, if you go on
turning round like that.

ALICE

How *can* she knit with so many? She gets more and
more like a porcupine every minute.

SHEEP

Now what do you want to buy?

ALICE

To buy! I should like to buy an egg, please. How
do you sell them?

SHEEP

Fivepence farthing for one . . . twopence for two.

ALICE

Then two are cheaper than one?

SHEEP

Only you *must* eat them both if you buy two.

ALICE.   Then I'll have *one*, please. (*Aside.*)   They

mightn't be at all nice, you know. (*She puts money on counter.*)

SHEEP

I never put things into people's hands . . . that would never do . . . you must get it for yourself. (*She sets an egg on the counter.*)

ALICE

I wonder why it wouldn't do? (*The shop gets darker, as* ALICE *pursues the egg.*) (* *16a.*) The egg seems to get further away the more I walk toward it. Well, this is the very queerest shop I ever saw!

SCENE 6

HUMPTY DUMPTY

(† 44.   * 17)

The EGG *gets larger and larger, and when she comes close to it,* ALICE *can see, as the LIGHTS come up, that it is none other than* HUMPTY DUMPTY, *sitting on a high, and narrow wall.*

ALICE

Why, it's Humpty Dumpty himself. And how exactly like an egg he is!

HUMPTY DUMPTY

It's *very* provoking to be called an egg . . . **very**.

ALICE

I said you *looked* like an egg, sir.   And some eggs are very pretty, you know.

HUMPTY DUMPTY

Some people have no more sense than a baby!

ALICE

" Humpty Dumpty sat on a wall:
Humpty Dumpty had a great fall.
All the King's horses and all the King's men
Couldn't put Humpty Dumpty in his place **again**."
That last line is much too long for the poetry.

HUMPTY DUMPTY

Don't stand chattering to yourself like that, but tell me your name and your business.

ALICE

My *name* is Alice, but . . .

HUMPTY DUMPTY

It's a stupid name enough!   What does it mean?

ALICE

Must a name mean something?

HUMPTY DUMPTY

Of course it must: *my* name means the shape I am . . . and a good, handsome shape it is, too.   With a name like yours, you might be any shape, almost.

ALICE

Why do you sit out here all alone?

HUMPTY DUMPTY

Why, because there's nobody with me! Did you think I didn't know the answer to *that?* Ask another.

ALICE

Don't you think you'd be safer down on the ground? That wall is so *very* narrow!

HUMPTY DUMPTY

What tremendously easy riddles you ask! Of course I don't think so. Why, if ever I *did* fall off . . . which there's no chance of . . . but *if* I did . . . *If* I did fall, *the King has promised me*—ah, you may turn pale, if you like! You didn't think I was going to say that, did you? *The King has promised me with his very own mouth* . . . to . . . to . . .

ALICE

To send all his horses and all his men.

HUMPTY DUMPTY

Now, I declare that's too bad! You've been listening at doors . . . and behind trees . . . and down chimneys . . . or you couldn't have known it.

ALICE

I haven't, indeed! It's in a book. (*Changing the subject.*) What a beautiful belt you've got on! At least, a beautiful cravat I should have said . . . no, a belt, I mean . . . I beg your pardon! (*Aside.*) I do wish I hadn't chosen that subject. If only I knew which was neck, and which was waist!

HUMPTY DUMPTY (*very angry*)

It's a *most provoking* thing when a person doesn't know a cravat from a belt!

ALICE (*in a humble tone*)

I know it's very ignorant of me.

HUMPTY DUMPTY (*relenting*)

It's a cravat, child, and a beautiful one as you say. It's a present from the White King and Queen. There now!

ALICE

Is it really?

HUMPTY DUMPTY

They gave it me, they gave it me—for an un-birthday present.

ALICE (*puzzled*)

I beg your pardon?

HUMPTY DUMPTY

I'm not offended.

ALICE

I mean, what *is* an un-birthday present?

HUMPTY DUMPTY

A present given when it isn't your birthday, of course.

ALICE

I like birthday presents best.

HUMPTY DUMPTY

You don't know what you're talking about. How many days are there in a year?

ALICE

Three hundred and sixty-five.

HUMPTY DUMPTY

And how many birthdays have you?

ALICE

One.

HUMPTY DUMPTY

And if you take one from three hundred and sixty-five, what remains?

ALICE

Three hundred and sixty-four, of course.

HUMPTY DUMPTY (*doubtfully*)

I'd rather see that done on paper. (ALICE *takes a pencil and paper out of her pocket and works the sum for him. He takes the paper and looks at it carefully.*) That seems to be done right ———

ALICE

You're holding it upside down!

HUMPTY DUMPTY

To be sure I was! I thought it looked a little queer. As I was saying, that *seems* to be done right—though I haven't time to look it over thoroughly just now—and that shows that there are three hundred and sixty-four days when you might get un-birthday presents. And only *one* for birthday presents, you know. There's glory for you!

ALICE

I don't know what you mean by " glory."

HUMPTY DUMPTY (*contemptuously*)

Of course you don't—till I tell you. I meant " there's a nice knock-down argument for you! "

ALICE

But " glory " doesn't mean " a nice knock-down argument."

HUMPTY DUMPTY

When *I* use a word, it means just what I choose it to mean—neither more nor less.

ALICE

The question is, whether you *can* make words mean so many different things.

HUMPTY DUMPTY

The question is which is to be master, that's all. Impenetrability! That's what I say!

ALICE

You seem very clever at explaining words, sir. Would you kindly tell me the meaning of a poem called " Jabberwocky "?

HUMPTY DUMPTY

As to poetry, you know, *I* can repeat poetry as well as other folk, if it comes to that . . .

ALICE

Oh, it needn't come to that!

HUMPTY DUMPTY

The piece I'm going to repeat was written entirely for your amusement.

ALICE (*sitting down, rather sadly*)
   Thank you.

HUMPTY DUMPTY
               I sent a message to the fish.
               I told them, " This is what I wish."

               The little fishes' answer was
               " We cannot do it, sir, because . . .

ALICE
   I'm afraid I don't quite understand.

HUMPTY DUMPTY
   It gets easier further on.
               Then someone came to me and said,
               " The little fishes are in bed."

               I took a corkscrew from the shelf:
               I went to wake them up myself.

               And when I found the door was locked,
               I pulled and pushed and kicked and knocked.

               And when I found the door was shut,
               I tried to turn the handle, but . . .
   (*Long pause.*)

ALICE
   Is that all?

HUMPTY DUMPTY
   That's all. Good-bye. (*BLACKOUT.* ALICE *crosses
   to right pinspot.*)

ALICE

Of all the unsatisfactory people I've *ever* met! Of all
the unsatisfactory people I've *ever* met!

SCENE 7

The White Knight

(† 45, 46 and 47.   • 18)

LIGHTS up. ALICE *finds herself in the woods once*
more, as the clatter of hoofs heralds the approach of the
WHITE KNIGHT *from the left.   He enters, riding on a*
white horse, crying " Ahoy!   Ahoy!   Check! " and
ALICE *sees that he is certainly not a good rider, as he*
tumbles forward and back and sideways on the horse.
When he reaches center, he falls off altogether, and sits
up, struggling to remove his helmet. ALICE *approaches*
him timidly.

ALICE

May I help you off with your helmet?   (*He nods his*
head emphatically, so she places one foot on his
shoulder, and pulls the helmet off.)

WHITE KNIGHT

Now one can breathe more easily.   (*He brushes back*
his shaggy hair and turns his gentle face and large
mild eyes toward ALICE, *whom he finds staring in open*
wonder at the little box he has fastened across his
shoulders, upside down with the lid hanging open.)
I see you're admiring my little box.   It's my own in-

vention—to keep clothes and sandwiches in. You see, I carry it upside down, so that the rain can't get in.

ALICE (*gently*)
But the things can get out. Do you know the lid's open?

WHITE KNIGHT
I didn't know it. Then all the things must have fallen out. And the box is no use without them. (*He unfastens it and is about to throw it away, when an idea strikes him, and he hangs it instead on a nearby branch just out of sight, off right.*) Can you guess why I did that? (ALICE *shakes her head. The* WHITE KNIGHT *is pleased.*) In hopes some bees may make a nest in it—then I should get the honey.

ALICE
But you've got a beehive—or something like one fastened to the saddle.

WHITE KNIGHT (*in a discontented tone*)
Yes, it's a very good beehive, one of the best kind. But not a single bee has come near it yet. And the other thing is a mouse trap. I suppose the mice keep the bees out—or the bees keep the mice out, I don't know which.

ALICE
I was wondering what the mouse trap was for. It isn't very likely there would be any mice on the horse's back.

WHITE KNIGHT

Not very likely perhaps. But if they *do* come, I don't choose to have them running all about. (*He pauses thoughtfully.*) You see, it's as well to be provided for everything. That's the reason the horse has all those anklets round its feet. (HORSE *shows off its anklets.*)

ALICE

But what are they for?

WHITE KNIGHT

To guard against the bites of sharks. It's an invention of my own. And now help me on. I must be on my way. (*As he starts to mount the* HORSE *evades him, and finally knocks him over. So the* WHITE KNIGHT *takes a ladder which is fastened to upstage side of* HORSE, *and placing it against the downstage side of the beast, mounts into the saddle. When he is at last properly seated,* ALICE *puts the ladder back in place. The* WHITE KNIGHT *turns to her solemnly.*) I hope you've got your hair well fastened on?

ALICE (*with a smile*)

Only in the usual way.

WHITE KNIGHT (*anxiously*)

That's hardly enough. You see the wind is so *very* strong here. It's as strong as soup.

ALICE

Have you invented a plan for keeping the hair from being blown off?

WHITE KNIGHT

Not yet. But I've got a plan for keeping it from *falling* off.

ALICE

I should like to hear it, very much.

WHITE KNIGHT

First you take an upright stick. Then you make your hair creep up it like a fruit tree. Now the reason hair falls off is because it hangs *down* . . . things never fall upward, you know. It's a plan of my own invention. You may try it if you like. (*He starts off, but the horse won't go in the direction he wants, which is off right . . . and presently he falls off again.*)

ALICE

I'm afraid you've not had much practice in riding.

WHITE KNIGHT

What makes you say that?

ALICE

Because people don't fall off quite so often when they've had much practice.

WHITE KNIGHT (*rising and going to* HORSE)

I've had plenty of practice; plenty of practice! (*He mounts* HORSE *from upstage side, by means of the ladder, and finds himself facing the tail.*) The great art of riding is to keep your balance. (*As he tries to turn himself around, he falls again.*)

ALICE

It's too ridiculous! You ought to have a wooden horse on wheels, that you ought!

WHITE KNIGHT (*lying prostrate, his head toward audience*)

Does that kind go smoothly?

ALICE (*laughing*)

Yes.

WHITE KNIGHT

I'll get one. (*Thoughtfully.*) One or two . . . several.

ALICE

How can you go on talking so quietly head downwards?

WHITE KNIGHT (*rising*)

What does it matter where my body happens to be? My mind goes on working all the same. And now I must leave you. (ALICE *fetches ladder, to help him on, but finds the* WHITE KNIGHT *is looking at her anxiously.*) You are sad: let me sing you a song to comfort you.

ALICE

Is it very long?

WHITE KNIGHT

It's long, but it's very, *very* beautiful. Everybody that hears me sing it, either it brings *tears* into their eyes, or else . . .

ALICE

 Or else what?

WHITE KNIGHT

 Or else it doesn't, you know. The song is called
" A-sitting on a Gate ": and the tune's my own invention.

> I'll tell thee everything I can;
> There's little to relate.
> I saw an aged aged man,
> A-sitting on a gate.
> He said, " I look for butterflies
> That sleep among the wheat:
> I make them into mutton pies,
> And sell them on the street."
> But I was thinking of a way
> To feed oneself on batter,
> And so go on from day to day
> Getting a little fatter.
> He said " I hunt for haddock's eyes
> Among the heather bright,
> And weave them into waistcoat buttons
> In the silent night.
> And that's the way " (he gave a wink)
> " By which I get my wealth . . .
> And very gladly will I drink
> Your honor's noble health."
> I thanked him much for telling me
> The way he got his wealth,
> But chiefly for his wish that he
> Might drink my noble health

And now, if e'er by chance I put
   My fingers into glue,
Or madly squeeze a right-hand foot
   Into a left-hand shoe,
Or if I drop upon my toe
   A very heavy weight,
I weep, for it reminds me so
Of that old man I used to know . . .
Whose look was mild, whose speech was slow,
Whose hair was whiter than snow,
Whose face was very like a crow,
With eyes like cinders, all aglow,
Who seemed distracted with his woe,
Who rocked his body to and fro,
And muttered mumblingly and low,
As if his mouth were full of dough,
Who snorted like a buffalo . . .
That summer evening, long ago,
   A-sitting on a gate.

And now I must be going. (ALICE *places ladder
against* HORSE.) But you'll stay and see me off? I
shan't be long. You'll wait and wave your handkerchief when I get to that turn in the road? I think
it'll encourage me, you see.

ALICE

Of course I'll wait: and thank you for the song . . .
I liked it very much.

WHITE KNIGHT (*as he mounts*)

I hope so. (ALICE *replaces the ladder, and brings
him his helmet*.) But you didn't cry as much as I

thought you would. (*He exits unsteadily, right. BLACKOUT.* ALICE, *standing in right pinspot, watches him a moment, and then waves.*)

ALICE

I hope it encouraged him. And now for the Eighth Square and to be a Queen!

SCENE 8

THE THREE QUEENS

(† 48, 49, and 50. • 19)

ALICE *finds herself, when the LIGHTS come up, seated between the* WHITE QUEEN *and the* RED QUEEN, *with a rope of pearls around her neck, a scepter in her lap, and a crown on her head.*

ALICE

What *is* this on my head? And how can it have got there without my knowing it? (*She lifts crown down into her lap and examines it.*) Well, this *is* grand. (*She replaces crown on her head.*) I never expected I should be a Queen so soon . . . and if I really am a Queen, I shall be able to manage it quite well in time. (*To the* RED QUEEN.) Would you tell me, please . . .

RED QUEEN

Speak when you're spoken to!

ALICE

—But if everybody obeyed that rule, and if you only spoke when you were spoken to, and the other person

always waited for *you* to begin, you see nobody would
ever say anything, so that ——

RED QUEEN

Ridiculous! Why, don't you see, child —— (*She
breaks off with a frown, and after thinking a minute,
suddenly changes the subject of the conversation.*)
What do you mean by " If you really are a Queen "?
What right have you to call yourself so? You can't
be a Queen till you've passed the proper examination.
And the sooner we begin it, the better.

ALICE

I only said " if "! (*The* TWO QUEENS *look at each
other.*)

RED QUEEN (*with a shudder*)

She *says* she only said " if " ——

WHITE QUEEN (*moaning and wringing her hands*)

But she said a great deal more than that! Oh, ever
so much more than that!

RED QUEEN

So you did, you know. Always speak the truth—
think before you speak—and write it down afterwards.

ALICE

I'm sure I didn't mean ——

RED QUEEN (*impatiently*)

That's just what I complain of! You *should* have
meant! What do you suppose is the use of a child
without any meaning? Even a joke should have some

meaning—and a child's more important than a joke, I hope. You couldn't deny that, even if you tried with both hands.

ALICE

I don't deny things with my *hands*.

RED QUEEN

Nobody said you did. I said you couldn't if you tried.

WHITE QUEEN

She's in that state of mind that she wants to deny *something*—only she doesn't know what to deny!

RED QUEEN

A nasty, vicious temper. (*There is an uncomfortable silence for a second or two. To* WHITE QUEEN.) I invite you to Alice's dinner-party this afternoon.

WHITE QUEEN (*weakly*)

And I invite *you*.

ALICE

I didn't know I was to have a party at all, but if there is to be one, I think I ought to invite the guests.

RED QUEEN

We gave you the opportunity of doing it, but I daresay you've not had many lessons in manners yet?

ALICE

Manners are not taught in lessons. Lessons teach you to do sums and things of that sort.

WHITE QUEEN

Can you do Addition? What's one and one and one

and one and one and one and one and one and one and
one?

ALICE

I don't know. I lost count.

RED QUEEN

She can't do Addition. Can you do Subtraction?
Take a bone from a dog: what remains?

ALICE

The bone wouldn't remain, of course, if I took it—
and the dog wouldn't remain: it would come to bite
me—and I'm sure I shouldn't remain!

RED QUEEN

Then you think nothing would remain?

ALICE

I think that's the answer.

RED QUEEN

Wrong, as usual. The dog's temper would remain.

ALICE

I don't see how ——

RED QUEEN

Why, look here! The dog would lose its temper,
wouldn't it?

ALICE

Perhaps it would.

RED QUEEN

Then if the dog went away, its temper would remain.

ALICE

They might go different ways.   (*Aside.*)   What dreadful nonsense we are talking!

BOTH QUEENS

She can't do sums a *bit*.

ALICE (*to* WHITE QUEEN)

Can *you* do sums?

WHITE QUEEN (*gasps and closes her eyes*)

I can do Addition, if you give me time—but I can't do Subtraction under *any* circumstances!

RED QUEEN

Of course you know your A B C?

ALICE

To be sure I do.

WHITE QUEEN (*whispers*)

So do I. We'll often say it over together, dear. And I'll tell you a secret—I can read words of one letter! Isn't *that* grand? However, don't be discouraged. You'll come to it in time.

RED QUEEN

Can you answer useful questions? How is bread made?

ALICE

I know *that!* You take some flour ——

WHITE QUEEN

Where do you pick the flower? In the garden or in the hedges?

ALICE

Well, it isn't *picked* at all. It's ground ——

WHITE QUEEN

How many acres of ground? You mustn't leave out
so many things.

RED QUEEN

Fan her head! She'll be feverish after so much thinking. (*They fan her with their scepters.*) She's all
right again now. Do you know Languages? What's
the French for " Fiddle-de-dee "?

ALICE

Fiddle-de-dee's not English.

RED QUEEN

Who ever said it was?

ALICE

If you'll tell me what language " Fiddle-de-dee " is,
I'll tell you the French for it!

RED QUEEN (*drawing herself up*)

Queens never make bargains.

ALICE (*aside*)

I wish Queens never asked questions.

WHITE QUEEN

Don't let us quarrel. What is the cause of lightning?

ALICE

The cause of lightning is the thunder —— No, no!
I meant the other way.

RED QUEEN

It's too late to correct it. When you've said a thing,
that fixes it, and you must take the consequences.

WHITE QUEEN

Which reminds me—(*she clasps and unclasps her hands*) we had *such* a thunderstorm last Tuesday— I mean one of the last set of Tuesdays, you know.

ALICE (*puzzled*)

In *our* country there's only one day at a time.

BOTH QUEENS

Poo!

RED QUEEN

That's a poor thin way of doing things. Now *here*, we mostly have days and nights two or three at a time, and sometimes in the winter we take as many as five nights together—for warmth, you know.

ALICE

Are five nights warmer than one night, then?

RED QUEEN

Five times as warm, of course.

WHITE QUEEN

Humpty Dumpty saw it too. He came to the door with a corkscrew in his hand.

RED QUEEN

What did he want?

WHITE QUEEN

He said he *would* come in because he was looking for a hippopotamus. Now, as it happened, there wasn't such a thing in the house that morning.

ALICE

Is there generally?

WHITE QUEEN

Well, only on Thursdays.

ALICE

I know what he came for, he wanted to punish the fish, because ——

WHITE QUEEN

It was such a thùnderstorm, you can't think ——

RED QUEEN (*aside*)

She *never* could, you know.

WHITE QUEEN

And part of the roof came off, and ever so much thunder got in—and it went rolling around the room in great lumps—and knocking over the tables and things—till I was so frightened, I couldn't remember my own name!

ALICE (*to herself*)

I never should try to remember my name in the middle of an accident! Where would be the use of it?

RED QUEEN (*to* ALICE)

Your Majesty must excuse her. She means well, but she can't help saying foolish things, as a general rule. She never was really well brought up, but it's amazing how good-tempered she is! Pat her on the head, and see how pleased she'll be! A little kindness—and putting her hair in papers—would do wonders with her ——

WHITE QUEEN (*with a deep sigh resting her head on* ALICE's *shoulder*)

I *am* so sleepy!

RED QUEEN

She's tired, poor thing! Smooth her hair—lend her
your nightcap—and sing her a soothing lullaby.

ALICE

I haven't got a nightcap with me, (*she smooths the*
WHITE QUEEN's *hair*) and I don't know any soothing
lullabies.

RED QUEEN

I must do it myself, then:
 " Hush-a-by, lady, in Alice's lap!
   Till the feast's ready, we've time for a nap:
   When the feast's over, we'll go to the ball—
   Red Queen, and White Queen, and Alice, and all!"
And now you know the words, (*she puts her head on*
ALICE's *other shoulder*) just sing it through to *me*.
I'm getting sleepy, too. (BOTH QUEENS *fall asleep*
and snore loudly.)

ALICE

What am I to do? Do wake up, you heavy things!
(*BLACKOUT.* **ALICE** *crosses down to right pinspot.*)
I don't think it ever happened before that anyone had
to take care of two Queens asleep at once! No, not
in all the history of England . . . it couldn't, you
know, because there never was more than one Queen
at a time. (*The* **WHITE RABBIT** *enters, right.*)

WHITE RABBIT (*in pinspot*)

Oh, my ears and whiskers! We shall be late!

ALICE
   Late for what?

WHITE RABBIT
   For the banquet.

ALICE
   What banquet?

WHITE RABBIT
   Your banquet, of course.   Quick now!   (*Pinspot out
   —complete BLACKOUT for a moment.*)

SCENE 9

THE BANQUET

(† 51 and 52. * 20)

*LIGHTS up. A banquet is in progress. Seated at
a long table are, from right to left, the* SHEEP, HARE,
DORMOUSE, HATTER, WHITE QUEEN, ALICE (*center*), RED
QUEEN, WHITE KNIGHT, *and* TWEEDLEDUM *and* TWEEDLE-
DEE *with a space between them, into which the* WHITE
RABBIT *presently comes, a fraction late, as usual.*

RED QUEEN (*to* ALICE)
   You've missed the soup and fish. (FISH-FOOTMAN
   enters left with LEG OF MUTTON. *To* FISH-FOOTMAN.)
   Put on the joint! (*To* ALICE.) You look a little
   shy; let me introduce you to that leg of mutton.
   Alice . . . Mutton; Mutton . . . Alice. (LEG OF

MUTTON *gets up in the dish and makes a little bow to*
ALICE.)   (* 20a.)

ALICE

May I give you a slice?

RED QUEEN

Certainly not. It isn't etiquette to cut anyone you've
been introduced to.

MUTTON

What impertinence! I wonder how you'd like it if I
were to cut a slice out of *you*, you creature! (* 20b.)

RED QUEEN

Make a remark; it's ridiculous to leave all the conversation to the mutton. (ALICE *is too bewildered to an-*
swer.)   Remove the joint!   (*The* FISH-FOOTMAN
removes the joint, off left, as FROG-FOOTMAN *enters,*
right, with the PUDDING.)

ALICE

I won't be introduced to the pudding, please, or we
shall get no dinner at all. May I give you some?

RED QUEEN (*sulkily*)

Pudding . . . Alice; Alice . . . Pudding. Remove
the Pudding. (*The* PUDDING *exits straight up in the*
air, [* 20c] *as the* FROG-FOOTMAN *exits right.*
Screaming.)   Queen Alice's health!

ALL

Queen Alice's health!

RED QUEEN

You ought to return thanks in a neat speech.   (ALICE *rises.*)

WHITE QUEEN

We must support you, you know.

ALL

To the Looking-Glass World it was Alice that said,
" I've a scepter in hand, I've a crown on my head;
Let the Looking-Glass creatures, whatever they be,
Come and dine with the Red Queen, the White Queen and me! "

(*During the following chorus, enter left the* KNAVE, *and* CARDS, *who bow to* ALICE, *and take positions flanking the forestage, and form themselves in two pyramids, right and left.*)

Then fill up the glasses as quick as you can,
And sprinkle the table with buttons and bran;
Put cats in the coffee, and mice in the tea . . .
And welcome Queen Alice with thirty-times-three!
With thirty-times-three!
With thirty-times-three!
And welcome Queen Alice with thirty-times-three!

(*All rise higher by standing on table.*)

' O Looking-Glass creatures," quoth Alice, " draw near!
'Tis an honor to see me, a favor to hear;
'Tis a privilege high to have dinner and tea
Along with the Red Queen, the White Queen, and me! "

(*During the above verse, enter, left, the* MOCK TURTLE,

the COOK, *the* DUCHESS, DODO, *and* MOUSE, *who bow,
and stand in front of* CARDS. *During the following
chorus, enter, down right, the* KING OF HEARTS *leading
the* WHITE KNIGHT'S HORSE, *on which is seated the*
QUEEN OF HEARTS, *still in a furious passion. The*
HORSE *bows to* ALICE.)
So fill up the glasses with treacle and ink,
And anything else that is pleasant to drink;
Mix sand with cider, and wool with the wine . . .
And welcome Queen Alice with ninety-times-nine!
With ninety-times-nine!
With ninety-times-nine!
And welcome Queen Alice with ninety-times-nine!

WHITE QUEEN (*seizing* ALICE *with both hands*)
Something is going to happen! (*BLACKOUT*.)
(* *20d*.)

ALICE
I can't stand this any longer! And as for *you*—
(ALICE *seizes the* RED QUEEN, *and is seen shaking her,
in the half light of the candles, as they shoot up to
the ceiling*) (* *20d*) as for *you* . . . I'll shake you
into a kitten, that I will. (*Candle effect off. Everything vanishes. The notes of the Boat Song fill the
air, and, presently,* ALICE *is seen at home again, curled
up in the great armchair by the fireplace, shaking the
black kitten* [* *20e*]. *She wakes slowly and looks
about, realizing that it was all a dream! She hugs
the kitten, and settles happily in the chair. . . . The
song continues . . . as . . .*)

THE CURTAIN FALLS

PRODUCTION PLAN

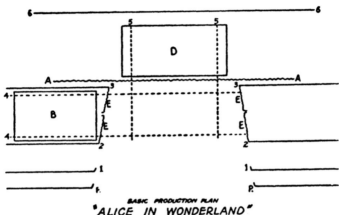

BASIC PRODUCTION PLAN
"ALICE IN WONDERLAND"
E. LE GALLIENNE

KEY TO BASIC PRODUCTION PLAN
Scale 1′ = ¼″

P to P. Proscenium opening varies with house.
1 to 1. First portal 30′ opening.
2 to 2. Second portal 28′ opening.
3 to 3. Third portal 25′ opening.
Distance between proscenium (P) and first portal (1) 3′.
Distance between first portal (1) and second portal (2) 5′.
Distance between second portal (2) and third portal (3) 11′.
A to A. Black velour traveller.
E to E. Black velour travellers travelling up and down stage.
6 to 6. Black velour backdrop.
B. Small wagon-platform 10′ x 14′. ─
D. Large wagon-platform 10′ x 20′.
4─4. Tracks for small wagon-platform 9′ 6″ apart.
5─5. Tracks for large wagon-platform 15′ apart.

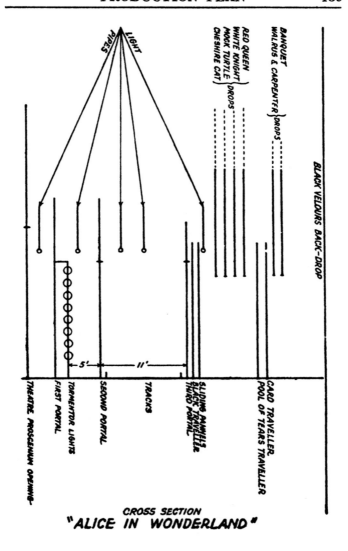

CROSS SECTION
"ALICE IN WONDERLAND"

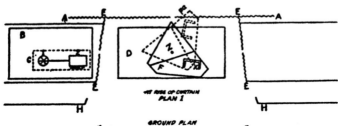

"ALICE IN WONDERLAND"

At rise of curtain travellers A—A closed. Travellers
E—E closed. Large platform D in its downstage position. Superimposed on it, a rotating piece F, on which
are set Alice's big chair, X, and triangular mirror and
mantelpiece unit, Z. The " real " mirror and mantelpiece († 2) and the " dream " or " Looking-glass "
mirror and mantelpiece († 3), constitute the long
sides of this triangular piece. When the rotating piece
F is in position for rise of Curtain as shown by solid
black line in Plan 1, above, the " real " mirror and
mantelpiece is forward.

    a.   On   cue   " It'll   be   easy   enough   to   get
         through . . ." rotating piece F revolves, and
         assumes position marked by dotted line F-a in
         Plan 1. This brings the " dream " side of the
         mirror and mantelpiece forward. Alice disposes
         of the kitten in a box between the two mirrors.
         The mirrors, themselves, are made of shimmer-
         ing transparent fringe.

(Offstage, small platform B is set for its first

move. Super-imposed on it is the special trick table platform C [dotted line], the winch which works the table, 1—the table itself, 2.)

(Across the forestage, below the First Portal, lies the scrim for the Pool of Tears, H—H.)

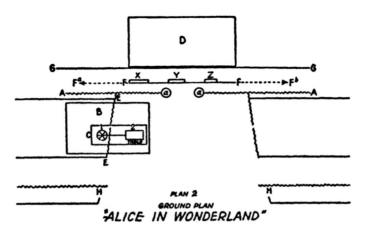

PLAN 2
GROUND PLAN
"ALICE IN WONDERLAND"

2. As Alice jumps down from the mantel, travellers A—A open, platform D moves to its upstage position, and travellers A—A close immediately in front of it. At the same time travellers E—E open, and Platform B moves onstage with trick table, 2. Travellers E—E close to mask winch, 1. (See Plan 2.) Immediately upon closing of travellers A—A, during Alice's discovery of the table that comes in on Platform B—the Little Door flat is put in position—F—F. This is a black velour flat with three doors appliqued on it—the large

door X, the fifteen inch door, Y, and the very small door, Z. This flat moves from side to side, bringing into position, a—a, whichever door is needed as Alice "grows" and "shrinks." After Alice's discovery of the key on the table, travellers A—A open to marks a—a, revealing door Y. This is the only door of the three which must be capable of opening.

a. While Alice is upstage center examining the little door, the bottle (and cake) is placed in position by mear⁓ of a grocer's "long arm" painted black, and invisible against the black velour travellers, E—E. As she comes down to the table travellers A—A close.

b. Specially constructed trick table grows, operated by winch. All travellers being closed, and the stage a solid mass of black, effect is that Alice is shrinking.

c. Travellers A—A open to a—a; door X exposed.

d. Travellers A—A having closed on door X when Alice returned to the table, have now opened on door Z.

e. As the table reaches its highest point travellers E—E open and platform B returns to its offstage position. Travellers E—E close.
   (Offstage platform C is removed from platform B, and platform B is set for Duchess' Kitchen.)
   (Note: Where lighting is adequate to mask the changing of the doors, travellers A—A

can remain open to points a—a, eliminating
the moves of travellers A—A, during door
changes.)

3. In preparation for the Pool of Tears scene—after
platform D is first moved to its upstage position
(* 2) and travellers A—A are closed, the Pool of
Tears traveller († 7 and 8) is stretched in
position G—G. (See Plan 2.) As Alice cries and
leaves the Little Door (X) for the last time, on
cue " The key! The key!" travellers A—A close,
and the Little Door flat is immediately removed.
Travellers A—A then open to their full opening
mark, exposing, as Alice falls into the Pool, the
Pool of Tears traveller, G—G. Simultaneously,
from below the first portal, H—H a scrim is raised
and kept at chin level. This scrim is opaqued at
the bottom, and painted towards the top to repre-
sent water. Two ripple spots are used in this
scene, one focussed on the traveller, and one, from
the front of the house, on the scrim. The light on
the scene is blue.

4. As Alice, the Mouse, and the birds step out of the
water, the scrim is lowered slowly, starting at its
stage left end, and the traveller travels towards
stage right, bringing into view the background for
the Caucus Race († 9 and 10). When this
background is in position G—G, the scrim is removed, and the lights brighten. On the exit of the
birds at the end of this scene, travellers A—A
close, and the Pool of Tears traveller is removed.

5. While Alice is in pinspot, on cue " He took me for

his housemaid," etc., travellers A—A open. Platform D passes through them to its downstage position, set with the Mushroom, and the door of the Duchess' House († 11 and 12). Travellers A—A close. Background for this scene is a flat attached to the platform.

    a. There are two pairs of 100 watt pinspots in the footlights, one stage right: and one left. They light Alice's face in blackouts such as this. Here, when she finishes her aside in the pinspot—on cue, " If I can find them " pinspot goes out and lights begin to dim up on scene at once, however, light has been so bright on Alice's face, she is not seen crossing to position. Effect is as of a dip of the lights.

6. On cue " He's perfectly idiotic! " Alice steps off platform D. Travellers A—A open. Platform D moves to its upstage position, and travellers A—A close. Travellers E—E open. Platform B moves on stage set with Duchess' Kitchen († 13). Travellers E—E close. The Cheshire Cat in this scene is a " profile " or " cut out," as inanimate as the stove by which it sits.

        (Offstage Platform D is being set for the Mad Tea Party, and immediately behind travellers A—A the Cheshire Cat flat is put in place, also iris spot and loudspeaker.)

    a. The pig is held by stage manager, offstage right, and is fed warm milk from bottle. In Blackout, Alice and stage manager change

doll and pig—then, when pig is set down it
runs off for more milk.

7. After the Duchess' exit, on cue "—play croquet
with the Queen," Travellers E—E open, platform
B moves to its offstage position, and travellers
E—E close. In Blackout for pig change, travellers
A—A open, revealing the Cheshire Cat flat († 15).

a. The Cat itself is painted on a transparency,
in an open space in the branches of the tree,
and only appears when lighted from behind
with an iris spot, which controls its appear-
ances and disappearances. Cat's voice comes
over loudspeaker placed behind its image.

8. While Alice is in pinspot, on cue, " Well, I've often
seen a cat ——" etc., travellers A—A close, while
Cat flat is removed and reopen immediately to
admit passage of Platform D on which the Tea
Party is set († 17), and then close again. As
in Mushroom scene, the background here is a flat
attached to the platform.

9. While Alice is in pinspot, on cue " It's the stupidest ——" etc., travellers A—A open, allowing passage upstage of platform D and the Garden
traveller is let in († 21 and 20).

a. Here, in the New York production, a moving
backdrop, traveller, or panorama, was used
painted with a repetition of rose-trees, fountains, and hedges from † 20 and 21. The
characters onstage made elaborate business of
walking, towards left, while remaining in one
place, as the background moved by from left

to right. Where practicable, this scene is effective. On the road, it had to be cut, proceeding straight to the croquet game, without any processional.

(Offstage during the following scene, platform B is being set for the Mock Turtle and Platform D for the Trial.)

10.   After the Queen's exit, during dialogue of Alice and the Gryphon in pinspot, travellers A—A close, and travellers E—E open to admit passage onto the stage of Platform B, set for the Mock Turtle († 25) and then close again.

a.   From behind a rock the Gryphon brings a hand microphone bedecked with a sea-shell, into which the Mock Turtle sings his song, in the manner of a " crooner."

11.   On cue from the White Rabbit, " The trial's beginning! " travellers E—E open. Platform B moves off left. Travellers E—E close. Simultaneously, travellers A—A open, and platform D moves on stage, set for Trial († 28). Travellers A—A remain open to reveal background for Trial which is a drop, let down as soon as the platform has passed through portal.

a.   While lantern, from first balcony, projects flying cards on stage and on Alice, Trial backdrop is flown. Platform D moves upstage, and Travellers A—A close in front of it.

b.   Card effect off. Lobsterscope from down right plays on Alice as she runs.

ACT II

12. On cue (business), Alice slowing down from run,
lobsterscope off, lights up, travellers A—A open,
revealing the Red Queen drop († 34).

> (Offstage, Platform D in upstage position,
> prepared for Walrus and Carpenter.
> Marionette Bridge for Walrus and Car-
> penter flown in above it, and breasted to
> floor. Platform B in offstage position, set
> with Railway Carriage.)

13. On cue, " Good-bye! " from Red Queen, travellers
A—A close. Travellers E—E open. Platform B
moves on stage set with Railway Carriage
(† 37). Travellers E—E close. Assistant Stage
Manager holds Alice's hat and cape for this scene.
In the Blackout, he hands them to Alice, who puts
them on while getting into her place in Railway
Carriage.

> (Offstage, the Red Queen drop is flown, and
> replaced by the Tweedledum and Tweedledee
> panels.

14. On cue, " That's some comfort," travellers E—E
open. Platform B moves offstage. Travellers
E—E close. Simultaneously travellers A—A open
revealing the Tweedledum and Tweedledee panels
(†38). The background for this scene is
painted on panels which separate in the center and
slide to right and left. As Tweedledum and Tweedledee find their places in the Blackout, they bring

the umbrella, used later, and place it behind them on stage.

a. The panels part revealing the set for the Walrus and the Carpenter († 39, 40 and 41). The rocks are placed on the forward part of Platform D which remains in its up-stage position and the background is on a drop which is let down behind them. The marionettes in this scene are operated from a bridge, which is flown in, above the front of Platform D, and breasted to the floor. The Walrus and the Carpenter may be either actors or marionettes. The oysters are marionettes. They act out the song as sung by Tweedledum and Tweedledee.

b. At the end of the song the panels close. (Offstage, Platform B is being set for Humpty Dumpty.)

15. This scene is played in front of the Tweedledum and Tweedledee panels. A flying track, between the first and second portals, should be used to fly the shawl and the Queen.

a. The shawl comes in on flying wire. When Alice catches it, the wire is drawn up out of sight.

b. The Queen comes in on flying wire, which remains attached to her throughout the scene.

16. During the White Queen's scene the Sheep Shop († 43) is set up on Platform D, behind the Tweedle panels. The Sheep Shop itself is built as a box unit, and occupies the stage left half of Plat-

form D. Behind window transparency a boxed-in flood light is placed on floor of Platform D. To the right of Platform D a black velvet panel projects from the side of the box unit, and on it are appliqued three luminous eggs of increasing size, the smallest being toward the center stage. At exit of White Queen the Tweedle panels open and Platform D moves to its downstage position. Travellers A—A close behind it. At end of scene on cue " I wonder why it wouldn't do " Travellers up-stage position, lights on the shop itself fade and A—A open, Platform D moves very slowly to its small pinspots from first pipe focus on luminous eggs one after the other. Travellers A—A close.

17. Travellers E—E, right, open. Platform B moves onstage, set for Humpty Dumpty († 44). Travellers E—E close.

> (Offstage, the Tweedledum and Tweedledee panels are removed, and replaced by the White Knight drop. Platform D is being set for the Banquet.)

18. On cue, " Good-bye! " from Humpty Dumpty, travellers E—E open and close for passage offstage of Platform B. Simultaneously travellers A—A open, revealing White Knight backdrop († 46). The White Knight's Horse is built on a wooden framework supported across the shoulders of two men who stand upright inside its structure; their legs in white tights, painted with Tenniel crosshatching form the legs of the horse.

Travellers E—E, left, open to admit entrance onstage of Horse, and close behind it.

(Offstage, Platform B is being set with
mantelpiece unit, and big armchair.)

19. As Knight exits, travellers A—A close. During
Blackout while Alice is in pinspot, the two Queens
enter with stool and props for Alice, and take positions center as in † 49. In complete Blackout
Alice finds her place on stool and puts on beads,
and crown she finds there, before lights come up.
All travellers closed for this scene.

20. On cue, "I don't think it ever happened before . . ." etc., while Alice and Rabbit are in pinspot, travellers A—A open on Banquet Table
(† 52), set on forward part of platform D, with
backdrop let in behind it. (For picture's sake the
background is much lighter than that of † 52,
and the table extends all the way across the front
of Platform D.) In the blackout the Two Queens
move straight upstage center onto platform D and
go through trap in center of table, taking Alice's
stool with them, and find their positions to right
and left of center, upstage of table. At the end of
Alice's dialogue with the Rabbit, she, too, in complete Blackout, goes through the trap in center of
table which is then let down, completing table, as
Alice takes her position at center of table. The
White Rabbit, at the same time, crosses off left,
and enters Banquet scene upstage left, as lights
come on.

a. Mutton is a marionette operated from the bridge, still in position from the Walrus and the Carpenter.

b. Actor speaking for Mutton is under table.

c. Pudding, also a marionette, is drawn up to marionette bridge.

d. As lights go out, lantern effect comes on with candles shooting upward like rockets to the ceiling, and caraffes flying about on flying saucer wings, as in † 52. All characters but Alice get down off table and disappear behind it, leaving her shaking the Red Queen, which is now a small marionette figure let down from bridge. On cue, " That I will," during complete Blackout, Travellers A—A close. Alice slips through them just before they close, is handed kitten . . . as . . .

e. Simultaneously, with the above, Travellers E—E open and close admitting passage onstage of Platform B set with mantelpiece unit. Alice takes her position in chair before lights come up.

ILLUSTRATION REFERENCE NUMBERS

(The illustrations by John Tenniel, which appear in all standard editions of the Alice books, are numbered here for easy reference in relation to the play. Corresponding numbers appear in the text and provide the key to background, costume, properties, and position of characters.)

ACT I

From " Through the Looking Glass "

1. Alice in the Big Armchair.
2. Alice going through Looking Glass.
3. Alice coming through other side of Looking Glass.
29. The March Hare as an Anglo Saxon Messenger.

From " Alice's Adventures in Wonderland "

4. The White Rabbit in Waistcoat.
5. Alice and the Little Door.
6. Alice, table, and " Drink Me."
7. Alice in the Pool of Tears.
8. Alice and the Mouse in Pool of Tears.
9. The Mouse addressing Birds, Animals.
10. The Dodo presenting thimble to Alice.
11. The Caterpillar on the Mushroom.
12. The Fish- and Frog-Footmen at door of Duchess' House.
13. The Duchess with her baby in the Kitchen.
14. Alice and Pig-Baby.
15. Cheshire Cat grinning in tree.
16. Cat, disappearing, all but his grin.
17. The Mad Tea Party.
18. The Hatter singing.
19. Hare and Hatter putting Dormouse in teapot.
20. Seven, Two, and Five of Spades around the Rose Tree.
21 The Queen of Hearts addressing Alice in the Garden, King, Knave, and Cards in background.

22. Alice and Flamingo.
23. Alice, Flamingo, and Duchess.
24. Reclining Gryphon.
25. Gryphon and Alice, seated, with Mock Turtle.
26. Mock Turtle, Alice, Gryphon, dancing.
27. White Rabbit dressed as Herald with Trumpet.
28. The King and Queen of Hearts holding court.
29. (See Act I, from " Through the Looking Glass,"
    above.)
30. The Hatter shaking out of his shoes.
31. The Hatter leaving the court, running.
32. King of Hearts with paper in hand.
33. Alice with flying cards.

ACT II
From " Through the Looking Glass "

34. Landscape—Tree and " Chessboard."
35. Alice and Red Queen standing.
36. Alice and Red Queen running.
37. The Railway Carriage.
38. Alice with Tweedledum and Tweedledee.
39. The Walrus and the Carpenter.
40. The Walrus and the Carpenter and Oysters (be-
    fore dining).
41. The Walrus and the Carpenter and Oysters (after
    dining).
42. The White Queen and Alice.
43. The Sheep Shop.
44. Alice and Humpty Dumpty.
45. The White Knight, wearing helmet (jousting with
    Red Knight).

46. White Knight, on horse with Alice at his left.

47. White Knight, falling off horse, with Alice at his right.

48. Alice, crowned.

49. Alice with Red and White Queens, awake.

50. Alice with Red and White Queens, asleep.

51. Leg of Mutton.

52. Alice pulling table cloth at banquet.

THE SCENE
Theresa Rebeck

Little Theatre / Drama / 2m, 2f / Interior Unit Set
A young social climber leads an actor into an extra-marital
affair, from which he then creates a full-on downward spiral
into alcoholism and bummery. His wife runs off with his best
friend, his girlfriend leaves, and he's left with… nothing.

"Ms. Rebeck's dark-hued morality tale contains enough fresh
insights into the cultural landscape to freshen what is essen-
tially a classic boy-meets-bad-girl story."
- *New York Times*

"Rebeck's wickedly scathing observations about the sort of
self-obsessed New Yorkers who pursue their own interests at
the cost of their morality and loyalty."
- *New York Post*

"The Scene is utterly delightful in its comedic performances,
and its slowly unraveling plot is thought-provoking and gut-
wrenching."
- *Show Business Weekly*

SNOW WHITE AND THE SEVEN DWARFS
Jessie Braham White

Fantasy / 24 characters / Various Sets

The handsome version of the famous fairy tale as presented in New York. Supposedly disposed of by the wicked queen, Snow White finds her way to a happy glen and the home of seven friendly dwarfs. A deadly apple casts her into a deep sleep, from which she is revived in time by her devoted prince.

TREASURE ISLAND
Ken Ludwig

All Groups / Adventure / 10m, 1f (doubling) / Areas
Based on the masterful adventure novel by Robert Louis Steven-
son, *Treasure Island* is a stunning yarn of piracy on the tropical
seas. It begins at an inn on the Devon coast of England in 1775
and quickly becomes an unforgettable tale of treachery and
mayhem featuring a host of legendary swashbucklers including
the dangerous Billy Bones (played unforgettably in the movies
by Lionel Barrymore), the sinister two-timing Israel Hands, the
brassy woman pirate Anne Bonney, and the hideous form of evil
incarnate, Blind Pew. At the center of it all are Jim Hawkins, a
14-year-old boy who longs for adventure, and the infamous Long
John Silver, who is a complex study of good and evil, perhaps the
most famous hero-villain of all time. Silver is an unscrupulous
buccaneer-rogue whose greedy quest for gold, coupled with his
affection for Jim, cannot help but win the heart of every soul
who has ever longed for romance, treasure and adventure.

THE OFFICE PLAYS
Two full length plays by Adam Bock

THE RECEPTIONIST
Comedy / 2m., 2f. Interior

At the start of a typical day in the Northeast Office, Beverly deals effortlessly with ringing phones and her colleague's romantic troubles. But the appearance of a charming rep from the Central Office disrupts the friendly routine. And as the true nature of the company's business becomes apparent, The Receptionist raises disquieting, provocative questions about the consequences of complicity with evil.

"...Mr. Bock's poisoned Post-it note of a play."
- New York Times

"Bock's intense initial focus on the routine goes to the heart of
The Receptionist's pointed, painfully timely allegory... elliptical,
provocative play..."
- Time Out New York

THE THUGS
Comedy / 2m, 6f / Interior

The Obie Award winning dark comedy about work, thunder and the mysterious things that are happening on the 9th floor of a big law firm. When a group of temps try to discover the secrets that lurk in the hidden crevices of their workplace, they realize they would rather believe in gossip and rumors than face dangerous realities.

"Bock starts you off giggling, but leaves you with a chill."
- Time Out New York

"... a delightfully paranoid little nightmare that is both more
chillingly realistic and pointedly absurd than anything
John Grisham ever dreamed up."
- New York Times

SAMUELFRENCH.COM

NO SEX PLEASE, WE'RE BRITISH
Anthony Marriott and Alistair Foot

Farce / 7 m., 3 f. / Int.

A young bride who lives above a bank with her husband who is the assistant manager, innocently sends a mail order off for some Scandinavian glassware. What comes is Scandinavian pornography. The plot revolves around what is to be done with the veritable floods of pornography, photographs, books, films and eventually girls that threaten to engulf this happy couple. The matter is considerably complicated by the man's mother, his boss, a visiting bank inspector, a police superintendent and a muddled friend who does everything wrong in his reluctant efforts to set everything right, all of which works up to a hilarious ending of closed or slamming doors. This farce ran in London over eight years and also delighted Broadway audiences.

"Titillating and topical."
- "NBC TV"

"A really funny Broadway show."
- "ABC TV"

Breinigsville, PA USA
27 January 2011
254281BV00005B/2/P